A NICE GIRL LIKE YOU

Lt. Andy Bastian is back for his second scintillating case. This time, he heads a gritting and gruesome search for the man who violated a teenage beauty and left her just intact enough to someday tell the tale. But when his best friend becomes the number one suspect in the case, Andy becomes one of the star legal attractions. Without an alibi, things look bad for Andy's friend — but can Andy offer to help him and keep his integrity intact?

Books by Richard Wormser
in the Linford Mystery Library:

PERFECT PIGEON
THE LATE MRS. FIVE
DRIVE EAST ON 66

RICHARD WORMSER

A NICE GIRL LIKE YOU

Complete and Unabridged

LINFORD
Leicester

First published in Great Britain

First Linford Edition
published 2019

*A catalogue record for this book is available
from the British Library.*

ISBN 978–1–4448–4082–7

Published by
F. A. Thorpe (Publishing)
Anstey, Leicestershire

Set by Words & Graphics Ltd.
Anstey, Leicestershire
Printed and bound in Great Britain by
T. J. International Ltd., Padstow, Cornwall

This book is printed on acid-free paper

1

Walt Adams called me at home. 'Listen, pal,' he said, 'Ellie tells me you're not coming to our party tonight.'

'Affirmative,' I said. 'I can't. Drew Lasley had to go to some sort of meeting of the gun club, and Jack Davis has had the duty three nights in a row; and anyway, he's chief, and he told me to take it tonight.'

Drew Lasley was day lieutenant, I was night lieutenant, and Jack was captain of the Naranjo Vista police department.

Walt said: 'You're killing me, pal. Ellie has invited the usual crowd of egg-domes, and there'll be nobody for a simple-minded high school principal to talk to.'

'Olga's going without me.'

I could hear Walt groan. 'Andy, I love your wife with all that is pure and noble in me. She is attractive, intelligent and sympathetic. But, lad, she is an egg-dome of the domiest. When it's just you and I and Olga and Ellie and maybe a few of the boys from the backroom, Olga is my dream girl, and if you weren't so big, I'd do something about it. But let her get where the ideas are flowing, and, man, she soars. What are you laughing about?'

'You,' I said. 'After all, couldn't you call yourself doctor if you wanted to?'

'A lousy Ph.D. in Education,' Walt said. 'Listen, I have to go to that gun club meeting, too. The sharp-shooters want to sponsor a junior rifle club in the high school. If I can talk your Lieutenant Lasley into taking over, will you show at my pad?'

I said I would, we exchanged a few more insults, and hung up. I was still chuckling. Walt Adams was right. Naranjo Vista was a-crawl with eggheads; we were a three-year-old, five thousand residence subdivision, and our main reason for being was to shelter the white collars from a couple of electronic defense plants. Of course that meant production men and purchasing agents and so on, but it also meant a large population of fellows who could split an atom as readily as I split infinitives, and Ellie Adams gloried in it. I, like Walt, have never enjoyed a conversation I couldn't understand. The executives and so on ignored people like Walt and me because we could do them no good. I had few friends in Naranjo Vista — just Walt and two or three more.

Olga, of course, was right up there. I once heard her talk for a half an hour on cybernetics, a word I have been unable to find in the unabridged dictionary.

Even if Drew Lasley didn't want to take the duty, I could go to the party. With our department as small as it was, it was impossible for a commissioned officer to be in the station twenty-four hours a day, seven days a week. Jack required that each of us work forty-two hours a week, and actually we each put in a lot more than that, but there are sixty-four watches in a week. I am not a drinking man, and I could go to Walt's party and still be on duty; I'd simply tell the sergeant on watch where to call me.

So I dropped Olga off at the Adam's and went down to the station to catch up on a little paper work until Drew got there, which would be the signal that Walt was home.

The paper work concerned three break-ins that we'd had in the last ten days. They looked like teenage stuff. In each case the icebox had been looted, cigarettes and liquor taken; but a damned fine transistor radio had gone out of one house, and that made it grand larceny, as well as breaking-and-entering.

County and state had sent me some M.O. files on known break-and-entry men and I studied them. An experienced criminal investigation officer, which I am, could do it at a desk; and I hadn't been working a half an hour before I was satisfied that none of the criminals known to be in Southern California had done our jobs.

Also, I was satisfied that the Messrs. Stern, Spratt and Thorne had all been victimized by the same person or persons.

Now all I had to do was catch said person or persons. I leaned back in my chair, wishing I had a pipe and a deer-stalker cap; this was one for the armchair detectives. Meaning, there wasn't much I could do.

The mark of a good executive — it says someplace — is a clean desk. It is much more important to get the cases off the blotter than it is to solve them. I picked up the phone and told Sergeant de Laune to get me Juvenile Division, Probation. This is an arm of the courts, and not a police organization at all.

At Probation, I talked to the switchboard; no use tying up our phones while they looked up my case number and got me the Probation Officer in charge. It turned out to be a Miss Virginia Bridge, a somewhat acid spinster I had dealt with before. By no coincidence, she was in the office. The load a Probation Officer carried, nighttime was the only time they could catch up on their office work.

She said she'd gotten the case from me and read it, but — 'My God, the case load I'm carrying — give me a minute to run over it — got it — yes. Three break-ins. What do you think, lieutenant?'

'Juvenile,' I said. 'Your pigeon, as they maybe say in England.'

'I read it that way, too,' she said. 'I've got it marked S & H.'

'That's a new one on me.'

'Son and heir,' she said. 'You can spot them a mile away. Those houses were almost undoubtedly robbed by kids living in them. Oh, my God, I don't know when I can get over to Naranjo Vista.'

'Don't look at me,' I said into the phone. 'You know the law. A police officer isn't supposed to mess with juveniles unless an immediate arrest is necessary to protect life or property.'

'You could go over to the school and read the riot act to them.' She sounded hopeful, but not very. 'I've got to go up to Tone this afternoon. I've got two clients getting out. I've got to be in court tomorrow. I've got a real messy one, teen-age prostitution, complete with a maid; she's an adult, thank God. The oldest girl is fourteen. That will be all day tomorrow. Yes, Andy, be a sweet, be a dear, go over to the school and bawl them out. How's Olga?'

'Leave my wife's name out of this. Sure, I can bawl them out, and if they call my bluff, where am I? We yell at juveniles, we don't even have a juvenile lockup where I can hold them for questioning. No, baby.'

She sighed. 'Ah, for the days of stupid flatfeet, who liked to yell at juveniles. Listen, Andy, would you do this? Ask your high school principal — Walt Adams, isn't it? — if all three of the homes have sons, and if they're the same age, and if they go around together.'

'Can do. As a matter of fact, Walt wants me to come to a party this evening.'

'Party!' Miss Bridge said. 'If I have time for a second coffee after dinner, I think I am living riotously . . . Do that for me, Andy. If all that's so, I won't have to hurry; unless they're feebleminded, they won't use the same stunt twice, not for a long time, and the peace and quiet of Naranjo Vista will not be disturbed.'

'Not to mention the law and order. Sure. I'll ask Walt tonight. If he doesn't know, I'll have Drew Lasley; he lectures there on traffic safety; just look in the files.'

'You're a darling. If I ever get an

evening, will you and Olga drive up to the city and listen to some records and eat some of my lousy cooking?'

She spared me another ten seconds for social chatter, and we rang off. She was, in a manner of speaking, an officer, but she was the kind of officer who has to have a couple of degrees in sociology, or something like it, to operate. She was much more of a pal of Olga's than of mine.

Finding it very convenient to have duty at Walt's house, I gave his number to de Laune, who would be on the desk till midnight, and told the sergeant I'd check before leaving there, and we discussed baseball, me without much interest. I don't know if he really cared about Los Angeles's chances to do this or that, or not.

At nine-thirty, Drew came in, in his second-best uniform. I was in plain-clothes. His lips were pressed tight together and his eyes were narrowed; ordinarily he is as good-natured as a cop can afford to be, but he was mad now. He signed the blotter without saying anything, and walked down the hall toward his office, his heels hitting on the linoleum or acrylic vinyl or whatever the Bartlett Construction Company had seen fit to floor our hall with. He heard me behind him and turned into my office, and started up and down it.

I was his superior by a tiny margin, and I was also official night chief. I went and sat behind my desk and said: 'Unload, pal.'

'You know Bailey Spratt?'

Spratt was the name on one of the break-and-entries, so I did. But it took me a moment to place him. 'Red-faced guy, about six feet, bulky; has a new-car agency over by the shopping center?'

'That's the bastard,' Drew said. He was ordinarily a mild talking man. 'Also president of the gun club, sergeant of the local squad of the sheriff's posse; a very big man, Andy.'

'All right, all right, what did he do? Ride you about not catching the varmints who robbed his icebox? I just checked that to Juvenile Division, by the way.'

Drew flung himself into the straight-backed chair at the side of the desk. Since I had chosen it to keep visitors from loitering, it didn't take to being flung into. I kept from grinning at the look on his face. 'Oh, that started it,' he said. 'He made a speech about it, in his official capacity as head of the posse squad.'

'But that was a gun club meeting.'

Drew Lasley picked up a pencil from my desk and snapped it between his fingers, tossed the broken ends into the wastepaper basket, without ever looking at what he was doing. 'All the posse men are also gun club members, of course. He also offered to take in, as special members, the other men in the club. 'Naranjo Vista needs men who can tell one end of a gun from the other',' Drew Lasley quoted, and looked as if he were about to spit on my floor. 'Also, he proposes to arm and drill special squads of high school kids, and that's where the trouble started.'

To me it sounded as if the trouble had started a good deal before that, but he was telling the story. I contented myself with asking: 'Was this because his house was broken into?'

'He said, and I quote: 'My house doesn't matter. I've got a gun and I know how to protect my property.' Unquote. But it seems a dozen other houses have been entered. It seems a decent woman's life isn't safe in Naranjo Vista, in her own home. It seems the police department has broken down, and it is time for the citizens to act, in the spirit of the old vigilantes, who made our great state what it is.'

'No,' I said. 'There'll be no gun-happy amateurs riding this town while I am second-in-command. I'm sure Jack feels the same way.' I reached for the phone book to get Bailey Spratt's number, then remembered something. 'According to you, you had not yet gotten to the trouble in your story.'

Drew Lasley said: 'The trouble is with Walt Adams. This Spratt loudsmouth wants all senior and junior boys in the high school to take an hour's drill a day in the use of firearms. Walt reared back like a .155 recoiling. It surprised me; I didn't know he had it in him. No kids in his school are going to be excused from classes for target practice, and if a high school gun team is started, they'll have to be under the supervision of a *paid* police officer. Spratt socked him. He'd make two of Walt Adams, but Walt got in one good wallop before he got knocked down. Then Bailey Spratt's pals held him, and Walt waved me away and walked out under his own steam. His face was pretty badly maced.'

'The high school auditorium is public property,' I said. 'You had every right to make an arrest.'

Drew Lasley shrugged. 'I'm Jack's assistant on the day watch, I'm traffic control officer, and I'm public relations man, but I don't set department policy. I had to keep telling myself that,' Drew Lasley said, and his face was a nasty red. 'Over and over I told myself that, to keep from removing Spratt's mastoids with my gun butt. Walt Adams is a damned nice little guy. But can we afford to start feuding with the citizens?'

'Since you reminded me I'm your

superior, you're off duty, by my orders. Go home and get drunk, or stay around and listen to me chew Mr. Spratt's tail.'

'Use your dullest teeth,' Drew Lasley said, which was pretty good.

After I dialed, the phone rang only three times before it was answered. I listened carefully as a man's voice said hello. There were masculine grumbles in the background; Bailey Spratt had taken his cronies home with him. Fine. If I had gone to his house, I would have had to humiliate him in front of his friends: over the phone, I could let him save any part of his face Walt Adams hadn't bruised.

'Mr. Spratt,' I said, 'this is Lieutenant Bastian at the Police Department.'

'I'm sure you're at the Police Department,' he said. 'You wouldn't be out patrolling after dark. The bogey man might get you.'

Drew got full marks, as our limey cousins say, for not gun-butting this jerk. But I was in my twenty-second year of police work; you learn to take it. 'We've got a full watch on duty tonight, Mr. Spratt,' I said. 'What I called you about was that little matter at the high school tonight. I can understand you're riled about having your house broken into; but that's no reason to give up your leisure and your sleep to patrol Naranjo Vista. Leave that to us, Mr. Spratt; we're paid for it.'

'Mister, I know you're paid for it. And my friend, the sheriff, is going to look into why you're paid.' Unless he had holes in his hand as well as in his head, he didn't bother to palm the mouthpiece as he called to his pals: 'I'm telling off one of those broken-down MPs at the police station.' Then he turned his valuable attention to me. 'We're taking over, and there's no stopping us. Law and order are coming back to Naranjo Vista.'

Taking a deep breath, I let him have it. I had been as patient as my oath required. 'Correction, Mr. Spratt. You are not, repeat not, starting a patrol. You are not, repeat not, going to carry guns on these streets after dark. You are not, repeat not, going to stop one pedestrian or one car, and if you do I will have you arrested and held the legal forty-eight hours for investigation.'

His voice was inarticulate on the other end. I caught snatches: 'Know who you're talking to . . . friend the sheriff . . . damned impudent cop . . . '

When he stopped for breath, I said: 'A little law, Mr. Spratt. Using one of those courtesy posse badges without direct orders from the sheriff, or in case of a crime committed before your eyes — and that's been held to apply only to felonies — can be construed as impersonating an officer.'

He didn't back down. 'In case of an emergency, copper?'

'There's no emergency here, Mr. Spratt.' I hung up. To my amazement, my hand was shaking, and I was breathing hard. It is difficult to make me lose my temper; Bailey Spratt had managed it. I said: 'Stand by, Drew, while I dictate a report on that call for the blotter.'

'I'll go down to the muster room and find the duty stenographer. Take a drink of water — or a drink — before he gets here. You did real good, Andy, real good.'

When I was alone, I calmed down a

little. I didn't think I'd done so well. There might be something wrong in the way we'd policed Naranjo Vista if it took me that long to calm down a citizen; there was something wrong if I couldn't calm him down at all without threatening him with arrest.

Maybe twenty years in the MPs didn't fit me for a civilian job. Of course, as constabulary in Germany, Egypt, Japan, and Korea, I'd had to deal with civilians from time to time; but usually they were enemy civilians in captured territory. Very different from guys who paid many grand for houses and felt they had hired you to protect those houses . . .

After I'd dictated my statement, with Drew kicking in stuff I'd forgotten, I told Patrolman Merril I'd sign it in the morning, and made Drew leave the station house with me. He'd wanted to stay on duty in case any of our cruisers ran into the vigilantes. But somehow I didn't think there'd be any amateurs on patrol for a while.

Now I know I should have called the sheriff and had him call his pal, Bailey

Spratt. But the county sheriff is a big office, and the job is held by a big politico, and I didn't want to bother him at home. Tomorrow I'd put the report on Jack Davis's desk, and he could take the whole thing up through channels to the sheriff.

Cops always stick together, I remember thinking; I'll be all right.

2

Some of the Adams's guests had walked to the party, so I was able to park my car fairly close to the house. As I crossed the front garden, so very much like ours, I could hear the party going full steam ahead, or up, or wherever parties go. I let myself in without ringing.

Ellie Adams, bent over a record player, looked up when the fresh air blew into the room, and waved at me. Then she bent over the records again.

I didn't see Walt anyplace. I threaded my way back to the kitchen, got a glass of quinine water so I'd look like I was drinking, and then, on an impulse, looked in the bedroom. Walt wasn't there. He must have gone to a doctor to have his face bandaged up, or maybe he was sitting in his office, brooding. I went back into the living room, a little worried. When I had a chance, I'd call him at his office, or tell a patrolman to cruise by

18

there. But the phone was hemmed in by guests, so I waited a minute for a clear field. Drew Lasley had said Walt walked out under his own power.

Over in a corner two men were arguing the Congo situation. There was absolutely no money to be made by joining them; I never understood the Congo situation, and I have a sneaking hunch nobody else ever did, either.

My wife Olga was arguing with an M.D. about the use of narcosynthesis, which was her business as a psychologist and his, I suppose, as a physician; but not mine. Police officers are forbidden by law to use the so-called truth serums.

Ellie Adams was presiding over the little group of rapt listeners near the record player. The record they were playing was atonal, dissonant and generally raucous.

It was a typical Naranjo Vista party. I drifted over to the bookcase and started looking at book titles.

Since a cop, according to most non-cops, wouldn't look at a book except in desperation, Ellie and Olga both broke off what they were doing and came toward me. But midway, Ellie got side-tracked by the phone, ringing.

My head came up; a call could be for me, but Ellie waved a finger at the doctor and he took it. As he started telling someone not to be alarmed, and to try two aspirin, Olga reached me and put a hand on my forearm. 'Andy, we can go home soon.'

'Don't be silly, Olga, I'm having a fine time.'

She grinned. Olga is not beautiful, taken feature by feature, and she simply doesn't give a damn about hair dos and clothes and so on, but she has the finest grin in the world. 'Liar,' she said. She looked around the room. Everybody there was a college graduate or better, and everybody there worked at the real high brain-level jobs — electronics, medicine, teaching.

I said: 'These are the taxpayers. Supposing they vote to try the Marxist system which, according to the Manifesto, states that when all citizens are economically secure and happy in their work, lawlessness will melt away and police will become unnecessary?'

Olga laughed, wholeheartedly. The doctor — his name, I remembered, was Harold Levy, and he was supposed to be a terrific medico — had finished his phone call, and joined us. Olga told him what I'd said. Just as he started laughing, too, the phone rang again, and both he and I swiveled our heads.

'Another of my patients with a splinter under the nail of his pinky,' he said.

But in a moment Ellie Adams said, 'You're wanted on the phone, Andy.'

The record she and her pals had been playing was an LP; super LP with extension. It was now going through a series of drumbeats, nothing else. But the room was reasonably quiet as I picked up the phone and said my name: 'Bastian.'

'Sergeant McRaine, lieutenant. I got a heavy one; better come over to Descanso and Walnut.'

'Right. Break-in?'

'Assault,' he said.

'Need a doctor? There's one here.'

McRaine said: 'No. I called the chief,

he said he'd bring some doctor that lives next door to him.'

A heavy case. Automatically, I looked at my watch, noted the time. Ten forty-eight. I started fishing my notebook out of my pocket; if you have to testify, the time is always important. 'Assault and battery, Mac?'

'Lieutenant,' McRaine said, 'it's rape. For God's sake, get over here.'

'Right,' I said, and hung up. McRaine was a tough one; he had time on a city police force before he came to us for reason of his kid's health. When he broke like that, it was bad.

Manners, Andy. I cut across the room, stood close to Ellie, and said: 'I've got to go, sweetie. Business. Thanks a lot, and I'm leaving the car for Olga.'

'Take it,' Ellie said. 'Walter will run her — No, Walter will be shot when he gets in. I'll take Olga home, or Hal Levy will.'

'Sure.' We were on Magnolia, one block over from Walnut; Descanso was three blocks away. It was an easy walk. But if I said that there was a big crime four blocks from her house, Ellie and all her guests might go with me. So I said: 'Tell Olga. I'll slip out without breaking up your party.'

I hadn't worn an overcoat to drive to the party in a closed car; to do so would be an insult to Southern California. But there was a uniform greatcoat in the back seat of the car, and a uniform cap.

Drew Lasley was out in the middle of the street at Walnut and Descanso, with a flashlight in his hand. 'Keep moving,' he said, 'there's nothing to see. Oh, it's you, Andy. Over there.' He waved the flashlight, unnecessarily, at a knot of men over in one of the rare vacant lots in Naranjo Vista. I could make out the burly figure of our chief, Jack David. In fact, I could see the captain's bars on his shoulders.

For all its thirteen thousand people and its five thousand families, Naranjo Vista had damn little police work. In the three years since the Bartlett Construction Company built the town, less than a hundred felonies had gone on the blotter.

I parked my car and crossed the street. Drew Lasley sneezed as I came near him. 'I'm going to get a great big whopping cold,' he said. 'I was in a hot tub when Mac phoned me.'

He was in full uniform. 'You must have dressed like a fireman.'

'Or a cop.' A car came along, slowed to see what was happening in the field. 'Keep moving,' Drew Lasley said. 'There's nothing to see.' The car went on and I finished crossing Descanso.

Jack Davis turned his flashlight on my face, and then pointed it down to guide my feet past a clump of fox-tails growing out of the raw red clay. He said: 'A real bad one, Andy,' and switched the light back to the center of the group.

An elderly man was just withdrawing a needle from a girl's arm.

It was a girl, all right; most of her clothes had been torn away, and her sex was clearly discernable. She'd been dressed in a sloppy-joe sweater and a plaid skirt. These were rucked around, but still on her; pink panties had been torn away, and so had a white bra, and her tan sandals had been kicked off; both her heels were raw from kicking on the ground.

As she relaxed from the needle, the doctor reached in his bag for cotton and made as though to mop up the mess around her middle.

Jack Davis said: 'No, doc. Lieutenant Bastian here'll want to do that for evidence.'

'Then hurry,' the doctor said. 'This girl should have a hot bath and be put to bed.'

Jack Davis said: 'Leatherwood left to get your evidence case when you got here.'

I said: 'There isn't much to do till I get the case. Fingernail scrapings, samples of the dirt under her. Whoever did it will have left traces on the clay . . . ' I knelt cautiously, and touched the girl's face. It was chilly with shock. 'Who found her?'

McRaine was — outside of Jack Davis — the heaviest man there. It was strange to hear his voice shaking in that bull throat. 'I did, lieutenant.' He usually called me Andy. 'I was just making a routine patrol. I turned my white light into the lot here and — ' He gulped, pulled out his notebook. 'That was at ten-thirty-six. She couldn't talk; I don't know her name. Radioed the station, Captain Davis relieved me at ten forty-one, sent me to the phone. Called Lieutenant Lasley and then had to phone the station to find where you were, sir, and — '

'All right, Mac, all right.' I bent over, not too happily. There was no doubt she'd been raped; the signs were plain enough.

Most of these cops would not have seen this very often. Jack Davis and I, with our experience in Occupation Force Constabulary, were hard to shock. I said: 'She looks like a high school girl. Mac, take a car — mine if you don't have one — and go back to that party I was at. Get Walter Adams to come here with you, for an identification.' It was a job for a patrolman, but Mac needed something to do.

Then I remembered that Walt might not be home yet, and, if home, might have landed in the Scotch bottle, and would be unable to come out. He'd had a rough time, being knocked down in his own high school. I said: 'If Mr. Adams isn't home, ask his wife who his assistant is, and get him here. I repeat, him. Work down the staff till you get a man's name. This is not a job for a woman.'

McRaine said: 'Oke,' and wandered away.

Dr. Barnhart looked after him, and said: 'He should have some sort of stimulant.'

Jack Davis said: 'He's got a daughter just about this girl's age.'

Dr. Barnhart said: 'She really shouldn't be lying there.'

I said: 'We don't have an ambulance. And I want to get my evidence on the site, before she's moved. There's an ambulance on the way from County Hospital, up in the county — '

Dr. Barnhart said: 'I am well aware of where the county hospital is, lieutenant. And I suppose you're right; if you took her home and there was a mother, she might go into hysterics, which wouldn't be good for the patient. But can't someone cover her?'

I took off my coat and laid it over the

cleanest parts of the girl. There weren't many.

Sirens were whining in the night, over toward the freeway that skirted Naranjo Vista. Dr. Barnhart said: 'That would be your medical examiner arriving. I was on my way to call.'

One of us said: 'Thanks a lot, doctor, and we'll call you if we need any testimony,' and he stepped out of the circle of light and was gone.

Jack said: 'Karinsky, go relieve Lieutenant Lasley out there. He'd better get back to the station. There'll be reporters and so on to handle.'

Karinsky had just finished his military obligation to his government, as being drafted is now called. He saluted and slapped his thigh with his palm to finish the flourish, did a real right about face and went away.

Jack and I were alone. He said: 'Andy, this is going to raise hell.'

'We can always go back in the army, captain. Run our twenties up to thirty years apiece and we'll get two-thirds pay instead of half.'

He chuckled slightly. 'Sure, sure. Only you're a major and I'm just a captain.'

We weren't calloused; we were cops. There was nothing to do till we got my lab outfit, till a medical examiner got there; there was no use beating our heads against the ground, there was enough blood now.

Somehow or other we should have prevented this; we were paid to keep Naranjo Vista quiet. City policemen are paid to catch criminals; in fact, a recent New York police commissioner made the rather startling announcement that crime prevention was no part of his department's duty.

But we were paid by the Bartlett Construction Corp, to make Naranjo Vista a safe, quiet place in which to live and enjoy life. The corporation had never balked at any expenditure we'd wanted to make. If Jack had asked for more patrolmen, stronger street lights, anything, we undoubtedly would have gotten it.

The girl lying on the hard, dry ground at our feet was our responsibility. I remembered something, suddenly. I had told Bailey Spratt that three break-and-entries are not necessarily the beginning of a crime wave. Now it looked as if I might have been wrong.

3

Bill Leatherwood got back before the state and county men. I had a manual in the kit; I opened it to the right page, and Jack Davis read off the check list to me. Quickly I filled little envelopes, boxes and jars with a variety of disgusting objects: earth, slime, blood, skin, hair. I took a couple of foxtails off the dried clump of wild barley; maybe a botanist could identify any we found clinging to a suspect's socks.

'Footprints,' Jack Davis said.

'None,' I said. 'It hasn't rained since last spring, and this is pure clay.'

'Red clay,' Jack said. 'Not too common.'

'Did you ever watch them build one of these ready-made towns? They pick up dirt from a highspot here, and dump it in a low spot ten blocks away. A surface geologist would go crazy studying Naranjo Vista.'

'Are there really guys called surface

geologists?' Jack Davis yawned.

'How do I know? Here comes the county and or the state. Wonder why the sirens?'

'Si-reens,' Jack corrected me. 'Whassa matta, you 'shamed of being a cop? Why, Andy, they have to blow their little horns to express themselves. After being polite all day to the taxpayers, they are all pent up.'

It was the county *and* the state, arriving in a dead heat. Their sirens moaned to a final stop, but they left the flashing red lights on; all around us, on Walnut and Magnolia, Oak, Lemon, Descanso and Monterey lights were coming on, windows and doors were opening.

They climbed out of their cars, and walked heavily toward us, the deputy sheriffs with their big guns low on their thighs, like old-time gunslingers, the SHP men neater, with their guns on Sam Browne belts.

If I had been a lawbreaker, I would have been terrified at all that artillery coming toward me, surrounding me. I would have screamed out a confession. In fact, it is funny that suspects don't scream out confession, when surrounded by ten or twelve guns, each holding six to eight bullets; but they don't. At least, I've never known one to.

Jack Davis said: 'Here we go,' and his voice dropped an octave, got a growl to it; a cop meeting other cops. 'Over here,' he said. 'I'm Chief Davis.' He turned. 'Leatherwood, you better go help Karinsky keep everyone away from here.'

Leatherwood went away. He left plenty of law behind him; they were shooting out their names and their ranks and their hands to be shaken like machine guns.

One of them was in plainclothes, with no visible gun. He'd have one, though, under his clothes, because he would be sworn personnel, just like me; a man who had taken an oath to uphold and enforce the law. I said: 'You from the lab? I'm Lieutenant Bastian, of the local force.'

'Yeah' he said. 'Sergeant Ernen. What we got?'

'Over here.' He followed me away from the crowd of uniformed men toward the girl. He said: 'Just a kid, huh,' and flashed his light at my case. I turned over to him my envelopes and boxes and bottles, all marked; he would take them to the county crime detection lab, and use his acids and reagents and microscopes and fluorescent lights on them and learn anything that had to be learned.

He said: 'You've done about everything that's to be done, lieutenant.' He looked at me a little curiously, perhaps wondering what a trained man was doing on such a hick force. 'Still,' he said, 'we'll make one more try.' He raised his voice: 'Jakens.'

Jakens was in plainclothes, too. He lugged a long cord our way, plugged in a light, yelled: 'Juice,' into the night, and heavy floodlighting hit the scene. All the big uniformed men came toward the light, but Ernen said: 'Hold it a minute, gents, we're looking for footprints.'

When he didn't find any, or anything else of any significance, he used a camera to photograph all angles of the scene, and called: 'Doc, it's all yours.'

The medical examiner said: 'You can take her away. Use Ernen's ambulance.'

He smiled. 'Been cold weather, you couldn't have kept her here. Makes it easier for you boys. I'll call your doctor — Barnhart? — and file a report tomorrow.'

A tall deputy rolled the girl on a stretcher, and started to pick the stretcher up. The edge of it caught on the deputy's big revolver and they had to start over again. Ernen had gotten a blanket from some place and threw it over the kid. I took my coat back, mopped at it with Kleenex. Not too bad. I put it on.

I said: 'Don't start your ambulance up yet; I still need an ident.'

Ernen said: 'You heard the man,' and they took the stretcher away. 'Quite a mob out there, lieutenant.'

'The sirens brought them. And the red lights.'

'Well, don't blame me . . . You go to FBI school? Me, too. Want to come see my rig? I laid it out myself. An old ambulance. I can do pretty near anything in the field — double microscope work, chemicals, I even got a darkroom so I can print and develop without going home.'

'Expensive.'

'You'd be surprised,' Ernen said. 'I did most of the work myself. No county in the state, not Los Angeles or anyplace, has anything like it.'

We walked around the knot of uniformed officers. They were just talking; there wasn't anything for any of them to do there, but of course, the press might arrive at any moment.

There were two ambulance-shaped cars. Jakens and the deputy were just stowing the stretcher in one; Ernen took my arm and led me to the other. I was interested; this was my business.

He'd done a good job. The inside of the hack was enameled white with several coats of enamel. The generator was at the back, so a man could stand up outside and start it by the weight of his arm. It was running now, giving juice to the floodlight and to the interior lights of the truck.

Ernen opened a drawer and showed me flat-out enlargements of every kind of cloth you could think of, raw silk down to the cheapest wood fiber imitation. There were prints of tire tracks, domestic and foreign, color charts of different brands of liquor. 'Hold up a labelled bottle to these, and you can tell at once if the liquor's been tampered with.'

I said: 'Man, you're good.'

'Sure. And I get the same pay as a sergeant who's learned how to ride a motorcycle without falling off. Still — '

McRaine stuck his head in the back of the rig. 'Lieutenant, I got your man here.'

'Thanks, Mac.' I didn't say goodbye to Ernen; he followed me out. Walter Adams, his face bandaged and his breath smelling of liquor, was standing by Mac. Olga and Dr. Hal Levy were behind him.

I looked at my watch; eleven seventeen. Thirty-five minutes since I had gotten the call. I said to Walter: 'Drew told me about your rhubarb. The department wants to thank you, pal.'

He gave me a wan look.

I asked Hal Levy: 'Did you bandage him up? This is a sort of rugged case.'

'He's all right,' Dr. Levy said. 'No concussion, no more shock than a highball could fix. The bandages are

37

mostly for cosmetic effect, as we trade school boys say.'

Still, I whispered to Ernen: 'Tell your man just the face. I don't want a fainting school teacher on my hands.' Sergeant Ernen slipped over to the other ambulance, and I took Walter's arm. 'Over here, Walter. Party over, Olga?'

'Hal and I thought we'd drive Walter back, so you wouldn't have to spare a man, I know how short-handed you are.'

Hal and I indeed. But I had work to do. 'Okay. Stay back, though, honey. This isn't too pretty.'

Olga gave her grin. I was always forgetting that, as part of her training, she had put in time as an attendant at the State Hospital for the Criminally Insane. She had seen plenty.

Walter was blowing clouds of alcohol that would have showed up brown on Ernen's charts. There was a dome-light in the ambulance, and Jakens and the blue-coated driver both held their flash-lights on the girl's face. I said: 'Take a careful look, Walter.'

He was shaking. 'What do you want of me? Why me?'

'Looks like a high school girl. I need to know her name.' I was using one of my professional tricks: a low, soothing voice. Walter Adams was about to blow up on me. It was smart of Olga, after all, to bring Hal Levy along; I could check Walter with the doctor, and get about my own duties.

Out where the light stopped, there were a number of citizens milling about. Walter rubbed his forehead and bent forward.

'She's — ' Walter gulped, started again. 'I think — Nora Patterson,' he said. 'Senior, business course.'

I looked at the driver and at Ernen's man to tell them to pull the blanket up again; and in the moment I had my eye off Walter Adams, the high school principal gave way; he grabbed my arm and started to go down.

He didn't hit the paving; I got my arm around him. Then Hal Levy was there. 'Let him go, Andy. Get him down to where we can raise his body over his head. He's just fainted.'

'The doc's gone,' Sergeant Ernen said. 'The medical examiner.'

'This is one of our local doctors, Harold Levy.'

Down at my feet, Walter Adams was losing a couple of dollars' worth of liquor into the township's gutter. Hal Levy was dexterous in holding him so the vomit didn't get on the clothes of either the patient or the doctor. I said: 'Olga, bringing Dr. Levy was the smartest thing you ever did.'

'Oh, I'm a help to you,' she said. 'I've had Walter spotted as a very unstable personality for a long, long time.'

Dr. Hal Levy looked up at me. 'If you don't need Adams any more, I'd like to get him home and under some blankets. He could go into real shock, between the liquor and all.'

'But we'll need him to go through the high school records,' I said, 'I've got to find out who the girl's family is, and so on.'

The doctor straightened up and gave me the wise, tolerant look a kindergarten teacher gives a pupil who has just failed

40

crayoning. 'Isn't there a key to the high school at the police station? I'm sure the school keeps its records alphabetically.'

'You're the doctor. Take the man away.'

Olga's eyes snapped at me; that was no way to talk to her friend, and to a professional man, too. The M.D. after Hal Levy's name demanded more respect from a peasant type.

She and Levy took Walter Adams away, back toward the doctor's car. Of course, I could have used Walt; I wanted to know who Nora Patterson's friends were, what boys she was seen with. But Walt would not have been in condition to help me much, anyway. He was probably about to pass out from the liquor that had gotten into his bloodstream before he threw up.

'The lady a doctor, too?' Sergeant Ernen asked.

'A psychologist,' I said. 'My wife.'

'That I could tell from the way she looked at you.' He laughed a little. 'I'll get rolling. The other car'll drop the girl at County. If you're up our way, drop in and see me. Don Ernen.'

'My first name's Andy.'

He climbed into the front seat of the lab rig, and drove off behind the ambulance.

I told McRaine to tell Captain Davis I'd be at the high school, and went back toward my car.

4

Beyond the police line made by Leatherwood and Karinsky and half a dozen
off-duty cops called out for the emergency, it looked as though all of Naranjo
Vista had gotten out of their two and
three bedroom homes to form a crowd.

For this, I had to thank the gun-hipped
deputies and their sirens. McRaine came
out in the street with me; I looked
around, and saw that none of our men
were wearing chevrons, so I told him to
take charge of the traffic detail. Drew
Lasley, by now, would have called all our
off-duty men in. Until I broke the case,
nobody in our department would get
much sleep . . .

Drew was at the station, the scientifi-
cally designed half of the building we
shared with the fire department. Mr.
Bartlett had told me once that his
architect had studied police departments
all over the world before drawing the

43

plans for ours. The building was, officially, a security control center.

A few reporters were already there; Drew Lasley was handling them. In plainclothes, I didn't stand out so they let me get back to my office. From there I phoned the patrolman on the front desk, and he got me the key to the high school. I told him to tell Lieutenant Lasley where I was.

Speed was now necessary. I wanted to tell Nora Patterson's parents what had happened to her before they heard it on the radio, or from a neighbor.

The high school was as scientific as the station: low, sprawling, with a maximum of sun and a minimum of distracting view in each classroom. I switched on the lights in the front corridor, and followed a sign of the offices. The third filing case I tried had the alphabetical files of students: Nora Patterson was not where she should be, and then I noticed that the files were broken up by classes; I had been looking at the freshman Ps.

She was there, all right. Nora Diana

44

Patterson, aged nineteen, born in Michigan — who was born in California? — business course. College of Intention (huh?) University of California at Berkeley. Parents: Norman, electronics designer at Thermolog, Inc., mother, Darlene, check clerk at the Safeway grocery . . .

'What are you doing here?'

I'd never heard her come in. She was a tall brown-haired woman, about thirty, in a camel's hair coat. Rather stupidly, I asked her who she was.

'Miss Crowther. I'm assistant principal. You're not supposed to be here; I saw the lights and came in. How did you get in here?'

'Police,' I said. 'Lieutenant Bastian, Naranjo Vista Police Department.'

She said: 'Oh,' and pushed her hair back from her forehead. 'Yes, I think I've seen you around. Didn't you make a speech to our assembly last month?'

'That was Lieutenant Lasley.' Drew and I didn't look at all alike, except we were both big men. I went back to my file folder. The Pattersons lived on Columbia Circle. A three-minute drive.

Miss Crowther said: 'Police or not, you have no right in our folders. Our students are all juveniles, their records are privileged from the courts . . . '

A lawyer yet. I said: 'Stow it, Miss Crowther.'

She gasped. 'Really! — Could I see your badge and your I.D.?'

'Yeah.' I started to get them out. When she saw my shoulder holster, she gasped again. What did she expect, a joke book? I laid badge case and card on the desk, and said: 'Just to fill out your legal background, Miss Crowther, some crimes are not privileged by age. For murder, for rape, juveniles can be tried as adults, and sent to the gas chamber if guilty.'

She had forgotten to look at my I.D. I said: 'I'm being deliberately brutal; I had to be to see if you could take it. You can. I'm in a hurry. A girl named Norma Patterson was criminally assaulted — raped — over near Descanso Drive a little while ago. I've got to go tell her parents about it. Want to come along? I could use a woman, in case Mrs. Patterson breaks down.'

46

She nodded briskly. 'Norma is a student clerk in the office here. Do you need that folder, or can I put it back?'

I handed it to her, and she snapped it back into the steel file, and closed the drawer while I re-stowed my badge case and my I.D. card. She took a brisk look around the office, snapped off the lights, and we walked down the hall in step.

Then she snapped off the hall lights, and we were outside. I locked the door and she tried the lock; a very efficient gal. As she straightened up, her hair passed near my nose; she didn't use perfume.

She said: 'I'll take my car and follow you. We might need them both.'

'Okay. Or if you'd rather, ride with me, and I'll get a police car to take care of you when you want to leave.'

She nodded again, and started toward my car. But when we were both in and I had put the car into gear, she said: 'It won't be a question of when I want to leave, will it? It'll be when you can spare me.'

'As soon as possible, Miss Crowther. It must be crowding midnight, and you're going to have a rough day tomorrow.'

The closest route to Columbia Circle would have been past Descanso and Walnut, but I detoured; it would be quicker if we didn't have to thread our way through the mob that was probably still gawking at the vacant lot.

'It is nearly midnight,' she said. 'I was at a movie up in the city . . . Yes, the kids will really be in an uproar tomorrow.' She laughed a little. 'We may have to call on you for a riot squad.'

'Our department doesn't run to such luxuries.' We were nearly to where we were going. I wasn't happy; what was about to happen was one of the worst duties a cop could draw. I should have sent a sergeant or a patrolman, but I don't interpret my oath that way. I said: 'Miss Crowther — '

She answered me, or she didn't — I didn't notice. Because just then some men stepped off the curbs, both of them, and waved flashlights at me, and my headlights picked up a car, without lights, rolling out of a driveway to make a barrier. I stalled the car, killed the lights, set the brake and jumped out, all in one motion, going for my gun.

They pinned me with their lights, and I could see they carried rifles. I was too badly blinded to see if they had hip-guns, too. I pretended to stumble, went to one knee, lunged forward and got the closest of them. I grabbed his rifle and dropped the butt on his toe, and when he went forward, I got him in a half-nelson with my left arm pulled against me, and my pistol stuck into his right side.

'All right,' I said, 'this is the police. Drop those guns and put your hands on your heads.'

They stood there, wavering. 'Guns down,' I said again. 'Hands up.'

One of them bawled: 'By God, it is a cop. I've seen him around.'

'Don't shoot, we're fellow officers,' one of them said.

'Then put those guns down.' Over my shoulder I barked: 'Lights on, back there.' I didn't want to tell them I had only a woman with me. But Miss Crowther got the word; the lights came on.

They had on badges all right — the

big, jewel-studded ones of the Sheriff's posse. They were laying their rifles — and one of them had a shotgun — on the pavement with the respect a man gives something he's invested too much money in. They each had a belt gun on, too, big pearl-handled .38s, standard with the damned posse.

'Over by that car,' I said. 'Put your hands on the roof, your feet well back. Weight on your hands.'

A thin, short man with bow legs drawled: 'Now, officer, you know us. You've seen our badges. There's no need for all these dramatics.'

I said: 'You are all lucky I didn't shoot first and count badges later. I want to see who you are. So far, I'm acting on the assumption you couldn't be responsible citizens; not and act like twelve-year-old hoodlums.'

They marched to the car; they lined up. Of course, I should have sent for help. It's not good practice to frisk four men singlehanded. But I was convinced they were exactly what they said they were. I was just putting on a show.

I took their hip-guns, added them to the weapons already stacked. Then I let them unbrace, and hand me their I.D. cards one by one. I made a big show of comparing faces with photographs.

'All right,' I said. 'Now, any of you sober enough to explain this?'

The thin man was named Joseph Harg. He said: 'We've none of us been drinking. We were just running a night patrol, keeping the peace here in Naranjo Vista. There's been a lot of crime.'

A lulu occurred to me; they don't often. 'To get a thief, set a thief. You figured to catch a bunch of teenagers by acting like them?'

Harg looked uneasy. 'We're not sure that kids did those break-ins,' he said. 'Anyway, we're a disciplined outfit. We're acting under orders from our sergeant. Bailey Spratt.'

The other three nodded.

I said: 'Okay. I've got your names. If my chief wants to charge you with interfering with a police officer, he'll do it. In the meantime, pick up your armor, and get off the street.'

They looked relieved. Joseph Harg said: 'Thank you, officer.'

'Lieutenant Bastian.'

'Thank you, lieutenant.'

I went back and sat behind the wheel of my car. As they drove off, Miss Crowther said: 'For a big man, you certainly moved fast.'

'I'm awfully well-trained,' I said. 'I've been at this since I was seventeen.' I started the car, went into gear. The taillight of the posse car was going around a corner at a nice legal speed. 'What were we talking about?'

'I don't know,' she said. 'You had just said: 'Miss Crowther,' in an inquiring sort of voice. My first name is Eleanor.'

I said: 'Eleanor, I'd like you to put your mind on Nora Patterson. What boys she went with, and so on. Her parents will be pretty good sources that way, but parents don't always know everything there is to know about a kid. I imagine nothing much happens around the high school you don't notice.'

'Flattery,' she said. 'However, it's true. Old maid schoolteachers live vicariously through the romances of their students. Is this the place? It's all lit up, so late at night.'

'Waiting for their kid to come home,' I said. I managed to suppress the sigh I wanted to give. My stomach was knotted and my hands were icy. I said: 'Listen, I had no right to ask you to do this. I should have phoned the public-health nurse; she doubles as matron when the department needs one.'

'Miss Hellman? She'd chatter your ear off.'

'Okay, but this is going to be as bad as anything that's ever happened to you.'

Miss Eleanor Crowther made a curious remark: 'That's what you think.' I almost didn't hear it; her back was to me and she was getting out of the car as she said it. I locked the bus and went around to join her.

We walked up a slab of curving cement, through azaleas and pyracantha and past a newly-planted deodar. The lawn smelled as though it had been freshly cut. The Pattersons took pride in their home; I was about to smash that home and their lives, and everything they cared about in the whole world.

It was ridiculous, but I felt guilty, as though by not going into that house I could keep the people in there from being destroyed.

So I shook my head, and took Miss Crowther's elbow, and went the last few feet to the steps, up three steps to the flagstone terrace, and across the terrace to the push bell, like a little soldier.

Eleanor Crowther said: 'This is hurting you, isn't it?'

'It's tearing my guts apart.'

'You're a funny sort of policeman.'

'We come all kinds.' That was enough stalling. I pushed the bell.

The door opened at once; they'd been waiting for a girl to come home again, but never the same as she'd left.

Mr. Patterson, Norman Patterson, looked more like a professional tennis coach than an electronics expert. He was in dark gray flannels and a white shirt, neatly tucked in and rising from a slim waist to firm, broad shoulders. His straight-nosed face was tanned under black hair without a touch of gray. He was about my age, a year or so on either side of forty.

He looked eager, then he saw us, and he looked not so eager. He said: 'Yes, what do you want?'

'Lieutenant Bastian, Naranjo Vista Police Department.' I held out my handsome blue and gold badge.

He stared at it as though its gleam were hypnotizing him. 'Very nice of you,' he said. 'But I told your man all there is to know over the phone. Nora was supposed to baby sit for the Nelsons, but she's never been there. She — '

'May we come in, please, Norman?' The use of his first name was not an accident; some cop about twenty years ago figured out it had a psychological impact. It impacted Norman Patterson out of the doorway, and we were in. I kept on with the dreary routine. 'Your wife home?'

'She's on the phone.' His hand made a gesture. I pushed Miss Crowther and she went in the direction the hand had indicated. 'I guess she didn't hear the doorbell, or she'd be here. She's phoning Norma's friends.'

Miss Crowther disappeared through the wide door to the left. I took a deep breath, and looked beyond Norman Patterson to the rear of the house. French doors back there opened out on a lanai — this was pattern C-3 of the Bartlett Construction Corp. — and the doors were flanked by hip-high alabaster horse's heads.

Norman Patterson turned to see what I was looking at, and said: 'We got those last summer in Mexico. Nora picked them out, so we made her tote them on the back seat of the car with her. They were awful to travel with.'

'Only child?'

He nodded, staring at me warily now. I think he knew what I was going to say; but like me, he wanted to put off the moment of saying.

No money was to be made by putting things off. I said, quickly: 'Your daughter is in the County Hospital. She has been raped.'

I put out my hand to steady him, but

he didn't want to be touched just then. He stepped back and stared at me with eyes that I had seen before — hating eyes, eyes looking at the bearer of the worst news in the world.

From inside the house a scream started, grew; broke like an overstrained heart. Norman Patterson turned and lurched toward the source of the racket.

So I trotted after him. The living room was light and airy and furnished in the Danish Modern manner. The woman sprawled over the phone, sobbing, had thin shoulders; the knobs of her spine protruded through the thin jersey blouse she was wearing. It was a singularly defenseless back, an almost childish back.

Norman Patterson kneeled and took his wife in his arms. I looked away. This was none of my business, but I had to stay there. I had to get information. My job was to catch a felon and turn him over to the district attorney; this was the place to start that job.

Miss Crowther was no place in sight. But then I heard her heels clicking as she crossed from one Navajo rug to another, coming down the long length of the C-3 living room. She had a glass of water in one hand, a bottle in the other.

She handed me the water, and shook three pills out in her hand. 'The bottle says two for sleeplessness, so I guess three won't be lethal.'

'No. Go ahead.'

She was very good. She tapped Norman Patterson on the shoulder, and when he looked up, she inserted her hands like a wedge between him and his wife. 'Here, Mrs. Patterson. Take these.'

'No, no. I have to go to Nora.'

'They wouldn't let you see her now.'

But Mrs. Patterson saw snakes in Miss Crowther's hands where I saw pills. She kept pulling away.

I turned on my bark. 'Your daughter's knocked out for the night. I saw the doctor give her the needle. Get your rest; she'll need you tomorrow.'

The old voice of command worked. She swallowed the pills, she took the water. Her throat twitched twice, and the sleeping pills were down.

Miss Crowther said: 'Come with me,

Mrs. Patterson,' but the lady had been ordered around enough. Mrs. Patterson said: 'Norman will need me — '

But her eyes were dimming. Miss Crowther handed me the bottle and said: 'You call the doctor.'

I almost asked her which doctor. Then I realized that I was a detective, and looked at the label. The prescription had been signed by Dr. Crory.

Not straining my education, I looked him up in the phone book. There was an office number, and an all-hours number; I tried the second one. It was a medical answering service. The girl there sounded noonish instead of midnightish. She said that Dr. Crory was not available; he was at the hospital in the city. Dr. Levy was taking his calls.

Hal Levy again, but that was not so startling; only four doctors, a dentist and a physiotherapist had rented offices in our Naranjo Vista. I said: 'Get me Dr. Levy, then.'

The girl said: 'Just a moment, I have a number for him,' and I heard the dial on her switchboard whirring.

The next voice was my wife's. Olga said: 'Yes?'

My throat felt tight. 'You all right, Olga?'

'Of course, Andy. Why?'

'Is Dr. Levy there? The answering service said he was taking Dr. Crory's calls.'

Norman Patterson came up behind me and said, roughly: 'We don't need a doctor. We don't need strangers in our house at all, at a time like this.'

'Afraid I'll have to be the judge of that.'

The phone said: 'This is Dr. Levy, lieutenant. I was just looking up something in one of Olga's textbooks.'

'I'm on Columbia Circle, family called Patterson. They're the parents.'

Hal Levy was fast as a cop. 'Of the girl who was — hurt? All right. I know the Pattersons, patients of Lonny Crory. I'll be right there.'

The phone was nearly back in its cradle when I realized he hadn't rung off; Olga was talking. I put the black object back to my ear: 'I didn't get that.'

'You want any help, Andy?'

'No. Miss Crowther from the high school is here; she seems adequate.' I rang off, aware that I had sounded stuffy and husbandly. But frankly, midnight was not the time I wanted my wife's textbooks looked at by a bachelor doctor.

When I turned from the phone, Norman Patterson was so close to me that I would have felt his breath if my mind hadn't been on the room at the other end of the phone. He had put on a jacket, a windbreaker. It took me a moment to recognize it; it was Army-issue, circa 1943.

One side sagged, and I needed no moment to figure out why. I was too close to him, by the judo manual, so I stepped back till the phone table bit into my thighs, before I made my lunge.

The pocket of the windbreaker tore, and I had his gun.

We stood, facing each other, breathing hard. He said: 'Give that back. A householder has every right — '

The night was filled with amateur lawyers. I said: 'Correction. Unless you have a license to carry a concealed weapon, this gun becomes contraband the minute you put it in your pocket. What were you going to do with it?'

His voice was high for such a virile man. I listened for a car out on Columbia Circle. I could use Dr. Hal Levy at the moment; this poor devil was about to fold. He was no nitwit, from his appearance or occupation, but the hardest mind has its limits.

'What the hell do you think I'm going to do?'

'Subjunctive: were going to do. Run out in the night and shoot someone, I suppose. Anyone.'

'No. What do you think I am? But a man's got the right to kill anyone who — who hurts his — ' He was breaking down fast.

But I am a cop. All day, all night, no matter how I hate it. I said: 'The law is handling things.'

'No jury would blame me,' Norman Patterson said, and went into his fold. He dropped down to the floor and buried his strong face in his long, straight fingers, and started crying, a horrible noise, like a wounded animal in a little cave.

Dr. Levy, kiss my wife good-bye and hurry.

More car noise in the street, but again it didn't stop. There was a curious and familiar rhythm to it.

Patrol. A car or cars were going around Columbia Circle in a regular rhythm, a ninety-second patrol rhythm. Drew Lasley, or Jack Davis, if he was back at the station and in command, must have gone nuts. We only had four cars in the whole department; we couldn't spare one for something like this . . .

The gun was still in my hand. I looked down at it. A Colt Woodsman's .22 . . . a target pistol, accurate and easy to aim as a pointed finger, but with no killing impact.

Norman Patterson was making sobbing, breathless noises on the floor. I dehorned the gun, dropped the cartridges into my pocket, and tossed the long, thin firearm on the foam rubber couch, while the car went by again.

Eleanor Crowther came out of the back part of the house. 'She's asleep.'

'Dr. Levy's on the way.'

She looked down at Norman Patterson and said: 'I don't suppose he'd take a sedative if I offered it. I'm glad it's Dr. Levy. He inspires a lot of confidence.'

'That's because he has a prematurely bald head and a big nose.'

Eleanor Crowther squinted her eyes at a hanging bubble-light across the room. They were, I noticed, green eyes.

'You're not a girl,' she pointed out, unnecessarily. 'Dr. Levy's very attractive to women.'

And he is a questing hound after textbook knowledge, day or night. 'If you say so, Eleanor.'

'What is that car doing, prowling around this house? It's been going on since I don't know when. Give me a cigarette, lieutenant.'

When I held the match for her, she put her hand on mine. Her nail polish was natural-colored, like Olga's . . . No, by God. Olga had started tinting her nails a couple of weeks ago . . .

Norman Patterson's sobbing had stopped. He got up off the floor, stared at us as though he'd never seen us before, and went over and sat in a slatted armchair made of whatever kind of wood Danes make chairs out of. His fingers plucked at the cloth over his knees.

I pulled aside the fiberglass window curtains and looked out. The circling car was two-toned, but not black and white, not a police car. Two men were in the front seat.

More posse men? I thought I'd scared all that back into its burrow. Jack Davis might have asked for county help, but then the men wouldn't be in an unmarked car. And anyway —

Another car came up, stopped, and Dr. Hal Levy got out. He reached back for the inevitable black bag, and then walked quickly through the Patterson's front yard.

I met him at the door. He said: 'How's Mrs. Patterson?'

'Knocked out. Miss Crowther's here, she got the lady to take three sleeping pills.'

Hal Levy said: 'Sleeping pill is quite a generic term.'

'Prescribed by Dr. Crory, doctor. Bottle reads take two; she's taken three.'

'I'll look at the bottle.'

Yet he was a nice guy; Olga and I were always running into him at parties and so on. He was just protecting his profession; he didn't like other people doling out pills.

I said: 'It's Norman Patterson, Hal. Without trying to diagnose, he looks like a bad shock case, and I'd like to question him.'

'We'll see if it's possible. First things first. The pills you gave Mrs. Patterson.'

They were on the phone table. He walked into the living room with me as I went for them. 'Olga said to ask you if you want your uniform. She could send it to the station in a cab.'

'No thanks, Hal. I'm making noises like a detective just now. Here's the bottle.'

He looked at it, smiled, 'Crory's quite old-fashioned,' he said, enjoying some quiet professional joke with himself. 'No, three of these won't hurt her. Where's Mr. Patterson?'

We had passed Norman Patterson

without arousing his curiosity in the least. I pointed, and Hal Levy turned to see the man sitting in his sleek chair, showing all the signs of idiocy.

Instead of going to Patterson, the good doctor gestured at me with his chin, and we walked down toward the lanai.

He said: 'I can give him a stimulant, and he'll be in good shape to talk to you. He'll also be in excellent shape to suffer whatever tortures a man in his position suffers. I can knock him out, and force him to get some rest. It's up to you.'

This wasn't fair of him. I compromised: 'I'll try and talk to him the way he is, and if it works, you can give him the sedative afterwards.'

'All right, but he's nearly in shock.'

Crouched on my heels in front of Norman Patterson, I put my hands on his knees. 'Norman, I hate to do this, but it's my duty. Who are some of Nora's friends? Boyfriends, particularly.'

'She's very quiet,' he said, clearly. 'She didn't go steady, as the kids call it. Muriel and I wouldn't let her. She is a very docile girl, very obedient.'

'Yes. But she went to dances and things. Who took her?'

'Oh, she could have her pick of any boy in her class. She is so pretty.' He was going from past to present tense with ease; I had seen this before. He knew his daughter would never again be a normal, quiet, high school girl, but he could only stand to think of it a moment at a time; then he would revert to the present tense and pretend she was untouched again.

But she wasn't; she might be a nervous wreck, or she might recover because of her youth, but she'd be a curiosity in high school, and they would probably have to move.

'Which is her room, Norman?'

He pointed at one of the doors, and I stood up. 'He's all yours, Hal. I can probably get as much out of dance programs and school annuals as he could give me. After all, girls are seldom assaulted by their friends.'

'How true,' Hal Levy picked up his black bag and opened it. As J went through the door into the room Norman Patterson had indicated, Dr. Levy had the

68

inevitable needle out.

Nora's room was not as austere as the Patterson living room. Her bed had a checked spread on it, somewhat like a French tablecloth, and the same red and white pattern had been carried out in the window curtains.

Her desk was clean cut, but she'd softened it with silly Japanese dolls climbing up each of the four legs. I thumbed her textbooks and notebooks first. But nineteen is a little old to be writing Nora Loves Osbert in schoolbooks. Then I went through the drawers of the desk for love notes or just notes.

Finally the mirror of her dressing table gave me three names of boys she'd gone to three successive school dances with. It seemed to me that this was abnormal, that every high school girl had a short spell of thinking some boy was the only one in the world, but it was unfamiliar territory for me.

I looked up to see Miss Crowther in the doorway.

'Getting any place, Andy?'

'Nope. Not really. I'll take you home.'

69

'Good. Miss Hellman's here; Dr. Levy phoned for her. We've got Mr. Patterson in bed. Have you looked in the school annuals?'

'No. A thought.' I followed her pointing finger to a row of blue-leatherette volumes in Nora's bookcase.

She'd been on the debating team, the girls' basketball team, she'd joined bowling, swimming clubs. She'd been secretary of her class one term . . .

In her pictures, she was pretty enough, but not the raving beauty her father thought her.

I said: 'She would have been almost twenty when she graduated. Isn't that rather old?'

'Not these days. People move around so much their kids lose a year or so transferring.'

'Oh.'

Eleanor Crowther said: 'What have you got, Andy?' and put one hand on my shoulder so she could bend over and look at the three annuals I had spread out.

As a freshman, sophomore and junior,

Norma Patterson had appeared in the front row of her class each time, being a rather short girl.

The books went back in the case. Out in the living room, Miss Hellman, the public health nurse, was spreading blankets on the foam rubber couch. She looked up: 'Good evening, lieutenant. Everything all right?'

What her definition of all right was, I didn't know. Nothing worse than a rape had happened, that I knew of. I said: 'Just fine, Miss Hellman.'

'I'll just sleep here,' she said. 'It really isn't necessary, but Dr. Levy, quite correctly I'm sure, doesn't like the idea of two patients under sedation and no one else in the house. Though Bartlett houses are quite fireproof.'

'Nevertheless, we have a fire department,' I said. 'Just like we have a police force and a public health staff. Live and let live, Miss Hellman.'

She looked at me as though I'd taken leave of my senses.

But I didn't bother to explain to her; why should I? I was a great big police officer, inspiring awe and admiration in everyone's heart; I explained to no man.

5

Miss Crowther and I went out and got in my car. She said: 'That was a mean crack you made to poor Miss Hellman.'

'Poor? She gets to live in Naranjo Vista, doesn't she? What greater bliss?'

'A husband,' Eleanor Crowther said. 'When she comes to the school, she sheep-eyes every bachelor teacher on the faculty. It's kind of pathetic.'

'How about you, Miss Crowther? Do you pine for married bliss?'

She turned on the seat and stared at me. 'My, you're in a nasty mood,' she said. 'Why?'

My breath came out of my chest with an intensity that surprised me. 'You are respectable,' I said. 'No night prowler. You, therefore, aren't aware that we've passed a great many more cars than I have ever seen out this late in Naranjo Vista, even on New Year's Eve. We must have seen a dozen of them. And here comes another.'

'I don't understand.'

'What every cop fears most,' I said. Now that I was talking about it, I felt better. Before, it had been like there was steam in my head trying to burst out. 'That barricade we ran into wasn't an isolated incident. The damned citizens are about to take the law into their own hands. Riot, Eleanor. Mob rule. Those damned county cops with their sirens told the people what is going on, what has happened.'

She waved a hand to the right, and I turned that way. We went under a street light, and I could see she was frowning.

As I stopped in front of her house, she said: 'But people have a right to know what is going on. They pay your salary, just the same way they pay me. I wouldn't have the right not to tell them what's going on at the school.'

'There's a slight difference,' I said. 'If they find out that the dear little children have been putting bubble gum on the teacher's chair, they aren't going to string

Junior up to the nearest flagpole.'

She said: 'Oh!' and put her hand to her mouth. 'But whoever did that to Norma. I mean — '

'You mean some lawyer will get him off. All lawyers are crooks, all judges are corrupt, all cops can be bought.'

She stared at me, and then slid out of the car, leaving the door open, and ran for her front door.

I switched on my spotlight and covered her. She had a very good figure, but I was not rubbernecking. There was a rapist somewhere in Naranjo Vista; I wanted to see her inside her house, with the door closed.

When all this had happened, I drove off.

In the next block I passed two more cars, each with two men in them; no women.

I headed for the Center, and the police building. Cars were parked all around our headquarters; an enterprising cop could have handed out a half dozen parking tickets. But I wasn't feeling enterprising.

Poor Drew Lasley could handle them;

Jack Davis was an experienced officer and by now an experienced chief; he would have ducked. So I drove slowly home; I'd call Drew from there, to let him know where I was.

There was nothing much I could do about tracking down the rapist. We'd get the known sex criminals file in the morning, from the state, from the county, from Los Angeles. We had none of our own.

While Naranjo Vista undoubtedly contained a few sex deviates, maybe more than a few — consult the Kinsey report — none of them had criminal records. So my men would run double patrols all night, and drop dead if they found the criminal attempting a second assault; but they would run the patrols because they had to do something.

And for the same reason, county and maybe state detectives — certainly Los Angeles men — would be out tin-earing the wino joints. This smelled like a wino job, the work of one of those desolate gutter-crawlers trying to make contact with the world they'd lost, the world of clean people and young girls.

Turning into my block, I cracked an approach to the case; I hadn't had any up till now. Get the boys out and question householders: had they employed any transient, unskilled labor lately, to cut a lawn or clean out a garage?

It might give us a description, but in the morning. We just couldn't afford to stir up the citizenry any more than they were stirred up tonight.

My lights flashed across the front of our house, and I swore. Should have had sense enough to turn them off; if Olga was sleeping with the living room door open, they'd lance right into the bedroom and wake her. And then — I'd dipped into her textbooks — I wondered if I'd left the headlights on just because I wanted Olga to be up, because I felt lonely and battered and needed her to comfort me.

The idea made me chuckle.

I left the car in the driveway because I might have to go out again, after I called Drew. But my Freudian musings caused me to walk on the edge of the lawn, rather than on the concrete driveway. I was self-conscious now about making noise; it would sound like a baby's wail for mama, at least to my own ears.

As I came up to the front door, I was aware of light on the immature hedge that was the opposite boundary of our opulent estate (no down payment G.I.). So Olga was either up, or had left the light on in the bathroom.

And then, as I reached my key out to the door, the light shifted, ever so slightly.

My gun was in my hand before I thought about it. I was off the little entrance porch, and crossing the lawn, moving easy, acutely aware of every little bush or shrub that might make me trip.

So I tripped over the hose, which I had left out. But I recovered without noise, and went on, and there he was, pressed against the side of our house, peering in the bathroom window.

Now I was doing what I knew best to do. Gun in right hand, pulled back so it didn't touch the suspect, so he couldn't whirl against it and knock it out of my grip. Legs apart, knees slightly crooked ready to bring up a heel if he kicked at my groin.

Left hand out, and on his collar, ripping him around with his back to me, slamming him into the wall, away from the window.

Voice hard: 'This is a police officer. Get your hands on that wall, higher, then lean your weight on them.' My foot went out, kicking his feet back till he'd fall if he moved a hand.

Gun in my left hand now, where he could see it as I stood in the light from the window, My right hand went over him, fast but thoroughly, frisking for a knife or a gun.

One, a knife. But, held in the light of the window, it wasn't a switchblade; it was an old boy scout type, a cheap one, and the largest blade was snapped off about an inch from the tip. An old break, since rust covered the fracture.

'All right, walk toward the car over there.'

His voice was weak and whiny, and the smell of cheap muscatel — they call it muscatoot in the cities that have Skid

Rows — was enough to gag a clean-living cop.

He said: 'Officer, I was just — ' and then he broke off, because even a wino couldn't explain what he was doing outside my window at one in the morning.

'Save it, bum, save it.' I don't like talking like that, but I don't mind it, either; it is sometimes the only way to talk. A quick confession, and Naranjo Vista could get back to striving in the sun. I felt pretty good.

My handcuffs were in the car. I got them out and slid them through the front bumper; there's a space there for the chain of a hydraulic jack that is just ideal for hand cuffing purposes.

'Lie down, bum.'

His whine rose to a wail. 'I was just wantin' to see the lady come out of the shower, was all.'

'Lie down, crumbum.' Maybe I should have said lay down. Anyway he got the idea, and sprawled on the concrete. I clamped both bracelets hard; I wanted him to suffer a little. Then I went into my house.

The phone was in the living room, but I passed it for the moment and opened the door of our bedroom, just as Olga opened the bathroom door and came out, rubbing at her hair with a towel, stark God-damned naked.

'How's about pulling down a shade once in a while?'

She blinked at me, too startled to say anything; she glanced at the bedroom shade, which was down all the way. She made no effort to cover herself, nor had she when we were first married; she was no prude. 'Andy, that's a fine way to come home. Did you bring a warrant for indecent exposure?'

'There was a man outside, staring through the bathroom window at you!'

She blinked, and then smiled: 'He must be hard up. I'm sorry, but the house on that side's empty, and anyway there's the hedge, and — I just never thought. You sound jealous, Andy.'

'There was a rape earlier this evening.'

She nodded soberly, the fun out of her eyes, and reached for a robe from the wardrobe that lined one side of our bedroom. 'I know. Of course. Hal told me. A girl called Nora Patterson.'

'He had a hell of a nerve, discussing police business.'

Olga sighed. 'Andy, I am a kind, sympathetic and ever-loving wife. But if you had a hard day at the office, you get three licks at me to get even, and no more. That was the third lick.'

Counting to ten never did me any good; I wonder if it ever helped anybody. I said: 'You could have been killed. Raped and killed.'

Her eyes grew wide. Then she gave her sober nod again, and suddenly broke into the grin I loved her for.

'Motive explained. You were worried about me. Freud would say you were sexually jealous, but pooh on old Freud.'

'Pooh on old Freud. The bathroom window's undoubtedly unlocked; it always has been. He could have waited till you came in here, ripped the screen out and — '

'All right, all right, I'm scared enough . . . Andy, he oughtn't to be running around in the night. There are other women and — he's the one, isn't he?'

'He's the one, all right. The chances of two sex maniacs running around Naranjo Vista in one night are kind of small. But he isn't running now; he's chained to the front bumper of our car.'

She shook her head. 'Oh, Andy. That's illegal, isn't it? I mean, it's almost a third degree. It gets cold out there at night. Couldn't you get into trouble, cruel and inhuman punishment, something like that?'

'Now you're worried about me. Or is it your unknown admirer? After all, it's quite a tribute to your charms — as you say, it gets cold out there.'

But her grin was absentminded. 'It makes me feel sticky, all over.'

'Okay, no more hardboiled cop jokes. I'd better go call in.'

Mike Egan, a day cop, was on the switchboard. When he heard my voice, he said: 'Hold it,' and gave me neither title nor name. While the switch was open, I could hear voices; the mess at the station house was not letting up. Then Jack Davis's voice came on:

'Where are you, Andy?'

'Home. It seemed a good idea to stay away from the station.'

Jack Davis said: 'Damnit, Andy, this is no station. It's a Civic Security Center.'

'My captain jokes. Jack — I got the bastard.'

There was a long silence. Then Jack Davis said: 'You're sure, Andy?'

And he had me stopped. All our years in military police, all our months in civilian work, all our background in crime hung somewhere in the air between me, here in my no-down-payment-G.I. house, and Jack, who was probably stashed somewhere in the Civic Security Center.

Finally I said: 'No, of course I'm not sure. How could I be, until a lab and a D.A. and a judge and a jury go through their tricks. But I never made a pinch yet that I was surer about.'

'Tell me about it.'

So I told him. And I didn't feel good while I was doing it. I felt like I was, somehow or other, betraying my marriage. And this would have to be gone through on a witness stand, too. A damned minor thing, but not to me . . .

When I finished, Jack Davis said: 'You have just run up the world's record for cheap and quick police work.'

'Luck.'

He said: 'Oh, sure. Of course. It always is . . . I'm in the firehouse, in case you wondered. The aroused citizenry hasn't thought of looking here for me. The Purloined Letter.'

'Huh?'

'A story in which a guy hid something in such plain sight that nobody saw it. Very literary. Aren't you glad you've got such a well-educated chief?'

'What are you jittery about, Jack?'

Our phone was in the living room. In the bedroom I could hear Olga moving around getting her clothes on. If this experience had given her a — conditioning? — against nudity, I was going to have a hell of a sanitation problem on my hands. I wasn't being very funny. I said: 'You still worried I've got the wrong man? It's too much of a coincidence, Jack.'

'Sure. But a coincidence is possible. And if I call off the search, and then this

85

guy is innocent — '

'Since Naranjo Vista opened, we haven't had a sex case, unless beating your wife for cheating is a sex case. Now, in one night, we catch two? Not a chance, Jack.'

He coughed, nervously. 'We've had peeping Tom complaints.'

'Captain, I'm waiting for orders, chief.' He didn't like being called chief; he wore captain's bars and thought of himself as a captain.

'Can you keep him in your house? I can sneak out through the back of the firehouse.'

'Jack — '

'I'll put the pinch on the air. I'll have Lasley let the citizens listen to it.'

'We'll be in my garage.'

6

Olga came out of the bedroom as I hung up the phone. Her lipstick was too bright against her skin; she was getting a reaction. I hated to leave her, but I wasn't paid to look after my own wife. I kissed her cold lips, and said: 'Gotta go, honey.'

'Just about to make coffee,' she said.

'There's a bottle of cognac in the sideboard, put a slug of it in.'

'Can't you wait?'

I shook my head. Then I said: 'If you hear noise in the garage, it's us, Jack Davis and me. We're going to question the suspect there.'

'Oh, can't you get him out of here?'

'He'll be mobbed if we show him anywhere near the station house. Lynched, maybe. I can't take a chance on that.'

'Lynching's too good for him,' Olga said. My Olga, the girl I loved — but, more important, the girl with the high,

high education — the B.A., the M.A. in psychology, the almost Ph.D.

My face must have shown what I was thinking, because she said: 'I shouldn't have said that. I guess I won't think it, in the morning.'

'Okay, kid. Another kiss?'

'Don't ask.'

The house door closed behind me, and I was out in the night. It was cold; there is not a night in the year in Southern California that doesn't get cold. And when the sun comes out, even if it is the dead of winter, you swelter. This is considered highly desirable, and thousands of people pour in every week to enjoy it.

The dome light came on as I opened the car door to get my greatcoat out. I put it on, and looked like a cop, on the surface at least. The handcuff key was in the inner pocket, in a little leather case.

My catch was chattering his teeth as I bent over him. His coat, as I slid my hand down the sleeve to find the cuff, was stiff and slick with dirt. I could smell the muscatoot on his breath, but it had worn off a little. I could smell him, too — sweat and food-stained shirt, body odors and the faint stench of rotten orange peels from the gutters and doorways he'd passed out in.

I un-cuffed one wrist and managed to get the nippers through the bumper without bruising him too badly. I didn't spare him for humanitarian reasons, but because I didn't want to mark him up. Sooner or later he'd have a lawyer.

I was helping him to his feet when a car came down the block. I pushed him down again, and got down with him. There was a spotlight on the car, but it would be thrown high, since it was being run by amateurs.

He said: 'What the hell?' His chattering teeth made it hard to understand him.

'Buddy, there's a lynch party out for you.'

The car went slowly by, and, as I had predicted, the spot played on the windshield of my car. I hauled buddy-boy to his feet again. He said: 'Who you tryin' to kid? Lynch party? Whata you think I am, a horse thief? I just wanted to see the lady with no clothes on. Nekkid. And, mister, you sure spent a lot of time in there!' He giggled, obscenely.

I hit him in the belly, and his stinking breath came flooding across me. He bent over, straining against the cuff in my hand.

Then he was sick, all over my driveway, almost over my shoes. His vomit smelt hardly any worse than he did; there was nothing in his stomach but half-oxidized sweet wine.

He straightened up, coughing, wiping his mouth on his sleeve. 'What kind of cop are you, anyway, talking about lynch parties, making me hide? I don't think you're a cop at all; I don't know what this is all about. So I done wrong, wanting to look at the lady — '

'She's my wife.'

It shut him up, but only for a moment. Then he giggled, his weak, alcoholic giggle. 'Old joke,' he said. 'That was no lady that was — '

He saw my fist balling, and shut up.

Finally, oh Lord, Jack Davis pulled into the driveway in his own car, not a department one. He flashed his spotlight once, and got out fast and came down to us.

'Thought you'd be in the garage.'

'When we tried to make it, a posse car went by. I ran into one before, and read them the riot act.'

'Those guys,' Captain Davis said. 'They think this is the Old West, or something.'

'After all, if they got any farther west, they'd get pretty wet,' I said. 'You bring my case?'

Jack shook his head. 'We'll take him in when it gets quieter.' With his car blocking us, we had less chance of being seen by a patrolling civilian. We went into my garage, pulling the big door up on its tracks, pulling it down behind us, standing in the dark until I had leaned the oil catcher up against the single side window. Then I pulled the light on, and Jack Davis looked my captive over. 'Throw him back,' he said. 'Under the legal limit.'

He got no smile from me. Nothing about this was very funny to me. But the truth was, this wasn't a very prepossessing criminal.

About thirty years old, but going bald; what hair he had was dark blond or maybe true blond with dirt in it. A scab on his forehead had dirt ground into it; when he opened his mouth to yawn — a sure sign he was afraid — most of his upper front teeth were missing.

His coat had been gray, once, his pants brown. Now dirt had them almost matching.

But the outstanding characteristic of my little dandy was that he was little. Not over five-feet two, maybe less.

So now you had the story of his life; he was small, and people picked on him, so he turned wino. He was small, and couldn't get a girl, so he took one, the rape way.

I could write the speech for the defense counsel, though he wouldn't want me to because he'd want to have a longer speech; mine wouldn't keep him in the limelight long enough.

Jack Davis said: 'We'll have trouble proving it to a jury. The girl's an inch taller than he is, at least.'

'He's a man, she's a woman. It gave him an edge.'

Wino whined. 'I don't know what you guys are talking about. I feel awful. You gimme pneumonia, an' I'll sue ya. I'll sue ya both, and the city, too. Hey, I'll get ten thousand dollars and — '

'Shut up,' I said. 'Take your pants off and hand them to me.'

His red eyes blinked. 'What is this, anyway? I ain't gonna take my pants off.'

Jack Davis moved his very burly shoulders. 'You heard the man.'

Wino giggled again. 'Hey, you got me wrong. You guys are queers, do it to each other. I don't go that route.' He pronounced it 'root', the civilian, educated way; Jack or I would have called it 'rout', Army, lower-class style.

'He's had a good start in life,' I said. 'College man, maybe. Bet there's a family someplace'll come up with money for a top-flight lawyer, when they hear baby brother's up for rape.'

The rheumy eyes widened. The semi-toothless mouth gaped. 'What are you framing me for? I look in a bathroom, and the next thing ya know — ' He mumbled along. His dialect swung from upper class to Skid Row and back again.

When he ran out of breath, I said: 'Take your pants off, or I'll do it for you.'

He took them off. I felt them, looked at them, sniffed them. Cop work. What makes our job so glamorous. I gave them back to him. I took out my notebook, noted the time, made an entry.

Jack Davis said: 'Yes?'

'Yes,' I said. 'There's half dried semen on his fly.'

Jack nodded. He said: 'It's my decision, I guess, whether to hold him in our station, or take him up to county.'

'What I saw of the county boys, I'd say hold him here. They have a good lab man, a Sergeant Ernen. The rest of them have guns on their hips, badges on their chests, and they use their heads to wear uniform hats.'

Jack Davis looked at our prisoner, and then at me. He was a chief of police, and he didn't like his lieutenant talking that way about other police officers in front of a suspect.

'I'd rather hold droopy here at our station.'

Wino had his pants back on, and mostly buttoned up. He didn't finish the job; he was shaking pretty badly. Jack Davis said: 'We ought to get a doctor for him.'

'We've got doctors in Naranjo Vista. With paraldehyde.'

Wino groaned. He had had the drug before, no doubt; it is given all alcoholics to prevent DTs when their liquor is suddenly cut off. None of them like it. I've never tasted it, but it smells like no one would like it.

Jack Davis said: 'What's your name, son?' I don't know what the son was for; just an Army-police habit, I guess.

Wino said: 'Davis, sir. John Davis.'

Any other time I would have let out a whoop at the punk's having the same name as the chief. But I didn't feel funny at all.

Jack Davis just grunted at John Davis and looked at me, daring me to laugh.

Instead, I said: 'What did you put on the air, Captain?'

Jack said: 'That a prime suspect had been arrested and taken to County Headquarters. It should have sent the nightriders to their beds.'

'If it didn't,' I said, 'there are two of us, trained policemen, to defend him. Let's get out of my garage and to the station. I want to call that Sergeant Ernen I told you about.'

Jack Davis said: 'It's about two in the morning by now. You think he'll be there?'

'Yes.' I was going on the fact that I would have been there; and Ernen was a lot more like me than I was like Jack Davis.

I cuffed little John Davis to my wrist, and we moved out; I noted the time for my log. There was no chance that this was a member of a dangerous gang who would make a furious assault to free him, but I noticed that Jack Davis moved his gun from under his coat to his topcoat pocket before we raised the garage door; I had my own side arm available, too.

That is the way to move a prisoner;

that, and no other.

We got into Jack Davis's car. He drove; the prisoner sat between us; I sat on the outside.

The streets of Naranjo Vista were quiet now. Here and there a light was still on in somebody's living room or bedroom; but the two-toned cars and the sports cars were all in their driveways or in the garages. Jack Davis lifted a heavy hand off the wheel and flicked a thumb at a lighted window. 'Somebody telling his wife what a hero he was,' he said.

'Our bosses.'

Jack Davis said: 'Sure.' He turned off Corona Circle, and we were in the homestretch; the lights of the station-house were dead ahead.

Little John Davis — I had better call him Wino Davis — said: 'It's the law that you guys gotta tell me what I'm charged with. You gotta — '

'Little man,' Jack Davis said, 'we don't gotta anything. But I don't mind; give it to him, Andy.'

'In educated language,' I said. 'Maybe he even is a lawyer, who knows? You are charged with a first degree felony, in that you committed criminal assault, i.e. rape, having intercourse with a female against her will, punishable by fifty years in state prison. Clear?'

Wino Davis said: 'Oh, my good God,' in the most cultured accent he'd used yet.

'Guilty or not guilty?' Jack Davis asked.

Wino Davis said: 'I spied on a woman, yes. On the officer's wife here. But she was quite all right when I was pulled away.'

'She's still all right,' I said. 'But the other one's in County Hospital.'

The little body squeezed between Jack Davis and me was shivering. But Wino was controlling the chatter of his teeth. He said: 'There wasn't any other one.'

I twisted around to look down at him. He had caught his lower lip between his teeth, was chewing on it. His filthy, scabbed forehead was wrinkled.

'We're not framing you, you know,' I said. 'We don't do things like that.'

He shook his head. 'I don't think you are,' he said, 'but it would be quite easy, you know. I've no money for a lawyer.'

'Where'd you go to college, Davis?'

He named one of the most respected universities in the East. I'm withholding the name in case I ever want to blackmail the alumni association. 'Only for a year, though,' he said. 'They fired me.'

'Ever been in the armed forces?'

The gutter, the Skid Row crowded back up in him. 'Aw, no,' he said. 'That's for the birds. Who wants to put on a uniform an' go marchin' around, totin' a gun?'

'Rejected as too short,' I said.

'Yeah. Wanta make somethin' of it? Lissen, you guys better go easy on me, I know a lotta things you wouldn't — oh, and I need a drink awful bad.'

Jack Davis twisted the wheel and cut the car into the drive of the station house; we dipped down and into the open-front garage where the department cars and the chiefs private car parked. Drew Lasley and the other cops and I kept our wheels in a parking lot behind the station.

7

Two rookies were washing the cars down. I am pretty certain that Scotland Yard does not expect its apprentice patrolmen to wash cars or do other menial work, but Jack Davis was Army-trained; sweeping floors and scrubbing windows was good for young policemen, just as it had been good for rookie soldiers.

They carefully paid no attention as we got in the big elevator — capable of carrying a stretcher and four men — and rode up one twelve-foot flight.

We'd taken three steps down the hall toward the chief's office when the newspapermen spotted us. They came charging up; lights went off, cameras clicked, all of them talked at once. The usual thing.

Jack Davis handled it in the usual way. He was big enough; I got credit for the pinch; no statement now, but he was pretty sure we had our man; more complete details in a half an hour.

The newsmen looked very happy. They were third or fourth stringers left here in the bare possibility that the criminal might be picked up in Naranjo Vista. The big shots would have passed on to the county seat or to Los Angeles.

Now the little guys had the story; and since most of them weren't even on salary, but were paid by the picture or the column inch, they were jubilant; and easy to handle.

They let us through into Jack Davis's office. I unlocked the cuffs and stowed them in my pocket. Jack Davis flipped the switch on his squawk box and told the duty sergeant: 'Bring Lieutenant Bastian's evidence case in here. And you better get us some hot coffee.'

Wino Davis said: 'Coffee ain't gonna do me no good. I gotta have a drink, chief.'

'Against the law,' Jack Davis said. 'No stimulants or narcotics . . . '

'You'd better get a doctor,' I said. 'Our pal is coming unstuck.'

The little man was bent over, his hands

clutching his solar plexus. He was muttering: 'Bottle in ya desk, know it, jes' one swallow . . . ' He had the dry retches, and in between spasms, he was muttering words that couldn't be understood. His face was a dull purple.

Jack Davis hit the box again and told the sergeant to get us a doctor.

We couldn't question him the way he was; we couldn't do anything with him. If I'd been alone, I would have maybe given him a drink; there was a bottle in my office, though I'm not much of a drinking man.

I suspect Jack Davis would have allowed the little man a snort, too, if he had been alone. But neither of us was going to say it to the other one, and so little Wino could suffer.

A patrolman, Leatherwood, brought in my evidence case. I could work on that. I pushed Wino Davis into a chair, took scrapings from his shoes, his pants, and so on and so forth; what with filling out the labels, it passed a good deal of time. I got his fingerprints, the hand I was not holding was twitching uncontrollably, classified them and gave them to the desk outside to be put on the teletype.

When I got back, Wino had slid to the floor, and was moaning there. Big drops of sweat had popped out on his forehead.

Of course, he wasn't as bad off as he acted, but self-pity is about the commonest characteristic of winos. This one was an expert at it.

Jack Davis sat behind his desk, looking disgusted. I couldn't blame him. I tried to feel sorry for Wino, but it was hard to do. He was a disgusting sight and a self-caused one. Maybe life had been hard for him, maybe it was unfair not to let him grow; maybe his mother hadn't nursed him long enough, or his father had not given enough deference to his three-year-old opinions.

But I had been raised in a poorly run orphan asylum, and both Jack and I had joined the Army at seventeen, more for economic than patriotic reasons. Poor Andy, poor Jack; but we didn't behave like little Wino Davis, retching on the floor.

More to get away from the sight than

anything else, I raised an eyebrow at Jack Davis's phone, and the captain nodded for me to go ahead. I asked the operator to get me Sergeant Ernen at County Headquarters.

Voices passed the word along, and then Ernen said his name and title into the phone. I gave him mine. He said: 'I was about to knock off and go home. Understand you've got the guy; I'll work up the evidence for the D.A. tomorrow afternoon.'

'Swell.'

'You're a good science man, lieutenant. Most of the specimens you collected read five by five. Any time they fire you down there, I could use you in the lab.'

'Well, thanks, sarge.'

'You sure you got the right guy? There's many a slip twixt, etc., etc.'

His voice sounded weary. Mine did, too. 'I'm sure now. After a good defense lawyer gets hold of me, I may shake a little. Suspect this guy's folks have money.'

'We catch them,' said the philosopher of the laboratory. 'Then if the courts let 'em go, it's not our fault. Short guy, is he? Mousy brown hair?'

'Right,' I said. 'Oh, we're not sure about the hair. It's too dirty to tell what the real color is.'

Ernen said: 'Yeah? That's funny. We come up with five buck a bottle hair tonic from under the girl's fingernails.' He no longer sounded sleepy; I no longer felt sleepy.

I said: 'You better give me what you have, Ernie.'

'Hold the phone, Andy.'

Cold sweat was forming between my shoulder blades. I held the phone while assorted noises came over it; paper rattling, static crackling, a click as his switchboard or ours checked the line for something or other. Then his voice again, businesslike and faintly worried: 'Suspect five-feet eight, give or take an inch. Weight, indeterminate. Age unknown. Wearing hair tonic, Lanolin base, grand Sussex, odor mixed floral . . . That's the manufacturer's description, Loot. Coat probably brown tweed, possibly imported. Trousers fawn flannel, pure wool. Beard black, curly . . . '

As I looked down at Wino Davis retching on the floor, nothing fitted. I said: 'Give me the beard again. How did you get it?'

'The victim,' Sergeant Ernen said. 'She scratched his face badly. Type AB blood, and dark hairs, almost black, not perfectly round, indicating his beard would have been curly if he let it grow. You know, beard hair is no indicator of top-of-the-head hair; she pulled a tuft, and it's medium-light brown, and straight.'

Still holding the phone, I reached down and grabbed Wino Davis's dirty, gritty hair, and pulled his face up so I could look at it. 'Wrong guy, sarge,' I said. 'We have the wrong guy. I'll want to get that on the air, fast.'

'Okay,' he said, very staccato. 'I'll give it to teletype from this end, too.' And he rang off.

Jack Davis was staring at me. I jiggled the hook. 'Sergeant, get out an APB. We do not, repeat not, have the suspect in the Patterson case. APB and urgent.'

Jack Davis said: 'You're sure?'

'Sure,' I said. 'This one checks out inches short, which I could overlook; those lab men with their angles of incidence and coincidence can get thrown on that. But our man has scratched jaws and cheeks, and this punk just has a scabbed forehead. You don't get whiskers off a forehead. And the man we want was wearing good clothes, it sounds like, and the wrong color and texture.'

Jack Davis sighed, deeply. 'Take him to a cell,' he said. 'The doctor can look at him there.'

I reached down and got a hand under Wino's armpit, hauled him to his feet. I felt awful. Our All-Points Bulletin announcing our catch had undoubtedly cooled down the search for the assailant of Norma Patterson. Maybe in some towns it was called off altogether. We shouldn't have been so fast.

But what could we have done? We'd had a duty to get the gun-toting citizenry off the street before they shot each other; we had a duty to calm the mob around the station house before they committed a crime in their gun-toting zeal. No situation involving a major crime is ever simple, and this one had been worse than most, because it was in such prime danger of becoming several felonies at one time.

The stairs to the lockup were in the other wing of the station; I hauled Wino down that way. He gave me no help at all; I was going to call ahead for a patrolman or a sergeant to take his other side, but he was such a little guy. I could have carried him in my arms, if I'd wanted to.

But he went fairly well with my arm around his back, my hand under the armpit farthest from me. I hated to touch him, filthy as he was, but I was sorry for the bad time we'd given him; sorry and feeling a little guilty. Maybe I had been oversore because it was my wife he'd been staring at.

We were approaching the front door and the desk that faced it. I took a firmer grip; whoever was on duty there could take over for me.

The front door opened, and two men came in. They weren't together, but they were so close that the second man got in before the door closed behind the first one.

The first one was Dr. Hal Levy. He blocked my view of the second one.

'What have we here, Andrew?'

'You sure are the open-eyed medico,' I said. 'Don't you ever sleep and let the competition — '

The second man had come around Hal Levy by then. Time slowed down, stumbled, almost stood still for me. The second man was Norman Patterson. He let out an unintelligible shout, and then I saw what he had in his right hand and I went for my own gun, and Hal Levy was swinging his medical bag, and we were both too late.

Norman Patterson brought up the pistol I should have taken away from him, and squeezed off a shot.

The miserable little body I was supporting jumped like a straw man on the pistol range.

Twenty-odd years of constant practice paid off. Before he could fire again, I had shot one of Norman Patterson's legs out from under him. As he fell, Hal Levy caught him on the head with the heavy black bag, and Norman Patterson was, for the moment, through.

8

Doors were opening and slamming, feet were running. Among the light blue shirts and serge coats of our guys, I saw the blue flannel shirts of the firemen; the shots must have boomed in their wing, too.

I could even hear Sergeant de Laune phoning: 'Get an ambulance rolling for the police department, Naranjo Vista. Code Two.' Code Two means red light and siren.

I knelt, slid a hand under Wino's shirt. He was slick with blood; when I pulled my hand out, it showed bright red — arterial. Hal Levy had dropped to his knees next to Norman Patterson. I called: 'Switch patients, Doc. I don't know how bad this one's hit; but Patterson has a hole in his thigh. I know just where to put the tourniquet on.'

Hal Levy jumped up, kicked his bag so it slid to me, and came over. As I passed him I already had my neck tie off. I bent, fumbled a fifty-cent piece from my pocket, and knotted it around Patterson's upper leg. The blood gushing out under his trousers stopped.

Hal Levy said: 'Not serious. Another inch and he'd have missed altogether. Why don't they shoot for the belly?'

He was ripping away Wino's filthy clothes with his ball-end dressing scissors. It was a good thing I had already checked the little fellow for evidence. I wiped my hands on Norman Patterson's trouser leg and lit a cigarette. Hal Levy said: 'This the bozo who raped the Patterson girl?'

'We thought so for a while, but he's not. I guess Norman Patterson here still thought so.'

Dr. Levy had come over. He used his scissors to look at Patterson's thigh. 'A couple of stitches in the artery and a week or so in bed — a very lucky shot. So he shot an innocent guy, huh? A policeman's lot is not a happy one.'

As he strolled back to pick up his bag and bend over Wino again, I wondered how many times I had heard that one, since I had become a seventeen-year-old rookie in an M.P. company. Usually, though, it was said by the cop. I wondered how many of the men who had said it knew it came from *The Pirates of Penzance*, by W. S. Gilbert and Arthur Sullivan, both later knighted.

I wondered how you addressed someone named Sir W. S. Gilbert.

I wondered a great many things.

Civilian clothes were mixed with the blue of the force, now. I asked Patrolman Leatherwood if Lieutenant Lasley were still around. He shook his head. 'He went home when you and the captain brought this fellow in,' he said. There was no use in getting him back. I could handle the press myself. I could handle anything; a very tough cookie, Andrew Bastian. And maybe when I got through handling everything, I could get a nice clean job peddling dishrags from door to door. I could handle that, too.

The human mind and the human frame are very resilient, and they persist in living, which means earning a living.

So I walked to my own office, followed

by the men in civilian clothes, the second-string reporters left to cover the tail end of our story, and now striking it rich.

Real newspapermen would have been easier to handle. These lads had studied their technique on television; they were automatically belligerent. 'Did you ever see your victim before?' 'Who was the man you were taking down the hall?' 'Is it customary for a lieutenant to personally escort a common drunk?' And so on and so forth, all coming at me at once, trying to machine gun me down.

For a moment I tried to answer them, but it was impossible; one strident voice would drown out the response to the question another strident voice had shot at me. I took out my side arm and pounded on the desk with the butt, something that should never be done with a pistol.

It silenced them. I said: 'We'll have a little order here, or I'll get in a couple of patrolmen and heave the whole bunch of you out on your ears. Then I'll call the Los Angeles News Bureau and give them a statement for all your papers, and leave you to explain why you couldn't cover a story.'

At once a flash bulb went off. I had an idea of how I looked, behind my desk, my damned gun in my hand. I said: 'Whoever took that picture can hand me the film, or be thrown out of this police station, and for good.'

They glared at me. Like most newspaper stringers, they doubled as both reporters and photographers; each had some sort of camera in his hand. There were four of them, though when they'd been shouting, they sounded like a platoon, instead of two very young men, a mannish girl of about twenty and a chubby guy in his forties whose straight hair straggled away from a bald dome.

'Get yourselves chairs, and let's talk this over,' I said. 'I want to issue a statement — I badly need to issue a statement — but I'm not going to be stampeded into saying anything I don't mean. Who took that picture?'

The girl said: 'I did. Betty Fordyke. I cover Hearst down here, and I work on the Shopping News, too.' She hesitated. 'I can't give you the picture, because it's on a roll of half-exposed film, but I can promise not to use it.'

From someplace down in my resilient middle I dredged up a grin: 'Okay, Betty. This office doesn't run to such luxuries as Bibles, so I can't ask you to swear.' Now I had them, they were all settling into the hard armchairs lined along my wall, getting ready to listen. I said: 'You all know my name, and I know Betty's, and I know you, Bob.'

Bob Myers was one of the kids. He covered high school football games for the only paper surviving in the county seat. The Chandler and Hearst papers in Los Angeles have wiped out most other daily journals in Southern California.

The fat man said he was Hal Freyer, and the blond youngster said he was Jim Kirby.

'I'm going to talk slowly,' I said, 'so you can all get this right, but if you prefer, I can get in a police stenographer, and have him make typed statements for you.'

They didn't know which was right; I

hadn't thought they would. They were very anxious to do what real reporters would have done. Finally Betty Fordyke said: 'I can take shorthand. If any of you miss anything, check with me.'

We were off. Enough time and enough words had been used up to take the fire out of them. I had dominated the meeting; but I wasn't very proud of myself. A man of my experience shouldn't have let it get out of hand in the first place.

'Tonight,' I said, 'as you all know, a girl named Nora Patterson was assaulted here in Naranjo Vista. Naturally, all the police of our small force were put on twenty-four hour duty, and we got aid from the county and from the California Highway Patrol, our only state police force. There was a good deal of excitement. A couple of hours after the discovery of Miss Patterson, I encountered a sex deviate in the night; I took him into custody.'

Hal Freyer smoothed his lank locks away from his greasy forehead, and said: 'Hold it, lieutenant. Do we get to ask questions now, or wait till you're through?'

'Shoot, Hal.' Maybe it wasn't the happiest of locutions.

'You encountered a sex deviate,' he said. 'What does that mean?'

'I encountered a man crouching in the dark, watching through a bathroom window while a woman took a shower.'

Betty Fordyke took up the cudgels: 'Oh, come now, Lieutenant Bastian. You mean, a man was passing by, saw a naked woman, stopped and looked and so you pinched him? I know men, mister; there isn't one wouldn't gawk at a thing like that.'

She had a very nasty way of saying she knew men. But if I lost my patience now, I was certainly in the door-to-door washrag business.

'Miss Fordyke, your analysis of male behavior is correct. I'd stop and look at the spectacle of a woman bathing with the shade up. No doubt you would, too. It's an eye-catching sort of thing. But to creep between a house and hedge and to peer under a shade raised perhaps one inch from the sill, is somewhat less normal.'

'But not enough to automatically classify a man as a deviate.'

Now I could let her have it. 'However, this suspect's pants were full of semen. In shorter and more vulgar words, Miss Fordyke — '

She was red as a beet. 'I get it,' she said.

'Then I'll continue my statement,' I said. 'Naranjo Vista was completed between two and three years ago. I have been on its police force all its life. In that time, we've had no sex crimes at all. Now, in one night, we had a rape and then I pick up a peeping Tom, and I don't mean a high school boy who watches the lady across the street get undressed.'

'All right,' Hal Freyer said, 'you've made your point. You've gotten your sadistic little kick out of embarrassing Betty here. Get on with it.'

'I had strong reason to suspect that I had picked up the man who criminally assaulted Miss Patterson. I secured my prisoner and called my chief, Captain Jack Davis. We gave this suspect a preliminary examination and then brought him into the station here.'

The high school reporter, Bob Myers was frowning. He was a nice kid. I said: 'Something troubling you, Bob?'

'Where did you examine the suspect?'

Now. 'In my garage,' I said. 'It was my wife he was spying on.'

They gasped. This put me right into the case, emotionally. They weren't good enough to dream up a real mess, but the papers they reported to had rewrite men.

And how they had rewrite men!

Betty Fordyke was back in the ring. 'Isn't it unusual not to bring a prisoner right into the station?'

'There was a good deal of local indignation about Miss Patterson being attacked. On the basis of more than twenty years police experience, Captain Davis and I decided to let it cool before subjecting our prisoner to a possible mob scene.' I raised my hand, very judicial, very official. 'Not that we couldn't have handled such a scene. But the mob, if one had formed, would have contained perfectly fine citizens, the pick of Naranjo

Vista. It seemed good sense not to have to have trouble with them. It still seems like good sense.'

Bob Myers, the youngest of the four, had the best brain. He said: 'You keep referring to the prisoner, the suspect. Did you get his name, lieutenant?'

'John Davis was the name he gave.'

That was really a bombshell. No reason for it, of course. Two John Davises is about as big news as two Tom Browns, two James Smiths. But crime and crime news is peculiar. Everybody was scribbling notes like mad.

'In the regiment where I first met Captain Davis,' I said, 'three of our officers and eleven of our enlisted men were named Davis. Three of them were named John Davis.' I reached for the Naranjo Vista phone book, thumbed it. 'Here are two John Davises and a J. W. Davis, and a J. L. Davis. John W. Davis was candidate for President once. I don't think he is the man we picked up.'

My audience was not exactly wowed.

'To continue,' I said, 'we brought this John Davis into the station. I called the county laboratory, to whom I had turned over various items collected on and about the body of Nora Patterson. Scrapings from under fingernails, the earth on which she lay and so on and so forth.'

'Very delicate,' Betty Fordyke said. 'Thanks.'

They were hostile. I had gotten them calmed, but they remained inimical. Nobody really likes a policeman, I had decided years ago, and you give a punk a chance to push a cop around, he's going to take it. These punks had the chance.

'The county police lab is in the charge — correction, I'm not sure he has over-all charge, but he has this case — of a Sergeant Ernen. Despite the late hour, the sergeant had already done a good deal of work on the specimens I had given him. This work definitely eliminated John Davis as a suspect.'

I stopped and took a deep breath. 'The rest you know. I was taking John Davis down the hall to book him as a drunk when Norman Patterson, who had heard that we had picked up his daughter's assaulter, charged into the station and shot Davis.'

'And you shot Norman Patterson,' Hal Freyer said.

'Mister, any time anyone shoots at a prisoner in my charge, I shoot back.'

At once I knew that my tone had been over-belligerent, too tough. They perked up; amateur newspapermen as they were, they still knew a good quote when they heard it. I'd given them a lulu to use against me.

Betty Fordyke said: 'And after shooting, you order the only doctor present to disregard your victim, and take care of your prisoner?'

It was a terrible effort not to lose my temper. I said, conscious of the patient note in my voice, physically unable to remove it. 'Dr. Harold Levy went at once to Mr. Patterson. I have shot several times in my military career. I hit where I aim. So I told the doctor to take care of Davis, who had an unassessed wound.'

Bob Myers said: 'Lieutenant, I think you're making too much of an effort to be accurate; the result is that you sound indifferent to the fate of the man you shot. I don't think you're doing yourself justice.'

He was half my age, and twice as smart as I. I looked at him gratefully, and said: 'Of course, I care. But caring, I've found, isn't worth much; my job is to do what helps, and to stay away when I can't help.'

Hal Freyer said: 'How many men have you shot in the course of your career, Bastian?' He looked at his fingernails — dirty — and yawned, as though the question bored him.

'Twelve,' I said, as quietly as I could. I watched them jump with surprise. 'Seven in the ETO, five in the Orient. Every one of them has been hit in the leg, and except for the very first, I've never shattered a bone. I am a professional, and not ashamed of it. When I aim at the fleshy part of the thigh, I stop the man I want to stop, and do him as little damage as possible.'

Betty Fordyke and Hal Freyer were scribbling furiously. Bob Myer was staring at me; it seemed I read pity in his eyes.

Betty Fordyke looked up from the hooks and eyes of her shorthand, and said: 'A general question, lieutenant. In England, policemen are not allowed to carry weapons. And yet, England's a well-policed country. Don't you think we'd be better off if we took the guns away from our cops?'

We'd also be better off if all bitches were kept in kennels. But I didn't say so. I took a deep breath, and made my speech. 'I've never cared for guns. I've shot target twice a month for more than twenty years, and I don't suppose you'll find anyone more accurate with a sidearm; but I don't like them. They're brain robbers. Too many people strap on a gun, and stop thinking; why think when you have all that power on your hip or armpit or wherever? England has laws about owning guns. We don't. Therefore policemen have to have guns; you can't handicap cops and let crooks go armed. It's as simple as that.'

Jim Kirby had said nothing so far. Now he came up with a lulu: 'What about the Sullivan Act?'

'A New York statute, Mr. Kirby, hardly applicable to California. I don't know of any western state that forbids the keeping of a gun in the home or carrying one unconcealed. Sawed-off shotguns and machine guns are forbidden, a statement that hardly applies to the present case. Mr. Patterson had every right to own the .22 Colt he shot John Davis with.'

Jim Kirby was blushing; I'd put him in his place. But Betty Fordyke's ears were — figuratively — wriggling. She said: 'You were twenty feet from Mr. Patterson, lieutenant. Could you tell he was using a .22 from that distance? A Colt?'

As a matter of fact, I probably could have identified it from that distance. But to say so was to evade the issue.

I said: 'I saw it earlier, in his house. He was going out to hunt for his daughter's assailant. I persuaded him to leave it to us.'

Hal Freyer stood up, shoved his copy paper in the sagging pocket of his sports coat and said: 'I got enough.'

Betty Fordyke stood up, jerked her girdle into place — I was surprised that she bothered to wear one, it certainly was not to make herself more attractive to men — and the two of them walked out without saying thank you, goodbye, or go-to-hell.

Young Jim Kirby said: 'Bob . . . '

Bob Myers said: 'Hang around, Jim, and I'll help you with your story. I want to talk to the lieutenant a minute.'

Jim Kirby gave me a grin and started out. He turned in the door, and said: 'That was a big blooper about the Sullivan Act.'

'The only people who don't make mistakes are the ones who don't do anything.'

He grinned again and walked out.

Bob Myers sat down on the edge of my desk and took a cigarette from my pack. He didn't light it, though; he juggled it on his open palm. Finally he said: 'Mr. Bastian, you couldn't have made more of a mess of that interview. Where was Drew Lasley? Isn't he press officer of your department?'

'We're a damned small force. Somebody's got to take the duty tomorrow.

Jack Davis sent him home to rest.'

Bob Myers shook his head. 'Why did you have to . . . It's done now. You had a squabble with Bailey Spratt earlier, didn't you?'

'Never heard of the lad.'

Bob Myers' hand closed and the cigarette squashed. He dumped it, paper, tobacco and all, on my carpet.

'He's president of the local gun club.'

'Then I did have a squabble with him, as you call it. Over the phone.'

'He's quite a politician. He belongs to everything — Little Theater, Episcopal Church, the Opera Guild and the Monthly Beerdrinkers League, for all I know. Lots of friends, lots of influence. He doesn't push around easy.'

'Cossack Bastian.'

'Exactly, pal. Listen. You need a public relations man. Me, in short.'

'I had another run-in with a posse squad headed by a Joseph Harg.'

'I know him,' the kid said. 'He's a chemist at Thermology. He went home and called Bailey Spratt and resigned from the posse. You were impressive.'

'It sounds like I don't need a press agent, then.'

Bob Myers shrugged. I had always liked him, but I didn't like the way he was looking at me now. 'Harg's a salaried man. Bailey Spratt is a big advertiser, for his car agency. You're going to get crucified.'

I said: 'And how much would you charge to make me nailproof?'

He stared at me. He looked mad. 'Two hundred a week till this dies down. Then — say — a hundred a month. In three years you'd be head of the Highway Patrol, or any other state police job you wanted. Cities would be competing to get you for chief.'

It was impossible not to laugh. 'How old are you, Bob?'

He made a vicious, knifelike motion with the hand that had messed up the cigarette. 'What does that have to do with it? I'll be twenty in a few weeks. I am a sophomore in the junior college. Next year I'm going to U.C.L.A.'

'Plan on making your million before you're of age?'

He hopped off the desk. 'Think it over, lieutenant. If you don't do something, you won't even be able to get back into the Army, except as a KP.'

'I don't have to get back in. I'm in the reserve as a major; all I have to do is apply for active duty.'

'The president is cutting the armed forces, the way I hear it.' He walked out of the office. He'd made his pitch and left the customer to think it over.

I had gotten down to the point where a twenty-year-old boy could blackmail me, I thought, as I left the office myself. I told the sergeant at the desk to call me if anything broke, and went outside; then I remembered I didn't have my car with me, and had to go back in and radio for a cruiser to come drive me home.

9

Patrolmen James and Sheel were manning the cruiser. They didn't speak all the way to my house. After they'd let me out, I wondered whether that was because they had too much respect to bother me, whether they didn't think it was worth their time to talk to a lieutenant who was going to be canned any day now.

Watching the taillight of their car go away, I decided it was the latter. I was in a lovely mood. Maybe I ought to sleep in the garage, for fear I'd beat up Olga.

Instead I went in, woke her up, and over a couple of cups of coffee in the kitchen, brought her up to date on events.

She said: 'Tomorrow, go to the sporting goods store and buy yourself a collapsible paddle and keep it in your pocket at all times.'

I said: 'Huh?' in my most brilliant fashion.

'You are up a deep, murky creek, Andy.'

'You're very funny.'

My wife shrugged. She waved a hand around. I noticed that the cuff of her bathrobe was frayed. 'We've got a three-year-old home and a two-year-old car. I've got six different changes of clothing, and before I knew you, everything I owned fit in one small suitcase. For a year I've been able to concentrate on studying without having to make my living. We're way ahead.'

'Just so we don't look back. Somebody's gaining on us. The house isn't paid for by twenty-odd years. The car isn't paid for, by twelve months. You're out of the habit of working, and anyway I don't feel like letting you support me.'

Olga looked at me, and then she suddenly gave that grin. She got up and walked across the kitchen and opened a cupboard and got out a bottle of brandy we'd bought when we were having important guests for dinner. Under the bulky flannel bathrobe, I knew that her figure was a little too thin, but otherwise just about perfect; under her usually grave face was always that grin; somewhere inside Olga was more guts than I'd ever encountered inside anybody.

Though I don't like liquor, I let her pour a slug in my coffee, a larger slug in her own. She didn't sit down again, but stood beside me, one hand on my shoulder and most of her weight on that hand. The other one held the coffee cup to her lips. 'Pal,' she said, 'nobody can ever make us forget that we once lived in a three-year-old mansion and drove a great big shiny new car.'

My arm went around her waist and my head rested on her breast, which was always surprisingly softer than it looked. 'God help the man who marries a psychologist. I ask for advice and comfort, and I get a dose of Edgar Guest.'

Her chuckle shook my head. 'You're getting the straight dope, my friend. Backed up by years and years of damned expensive education. You're yourself, Andrew Bastian; you're not a badge, a gun or a tailored blue serge uniform.'

'In other words, give them hell? Knowing he was right, the boy stood steadfast?'

She laughed again, and again I was jiggled pleasantly. 'Most of what you've done was wrong,' she said, blandly. 'But you did it, and no one else.'

The brandy was warming me, or maybe it was the coffee. 'Even Hal Levy called me lucky for putting that bullet where I did. I don't get credit for marksmanship.'

'Poor little Andy. Does he want a tin medal?'

'Go to hell,' I said. 'And talking of that, you and the good doctor Levy are getting mighty chummy.'

She nodded and moved away from me. She fished a cigarette and matches out of her robe pocket and lit up, walked up and down the kitchen, holding her left elbow tip with her right palm. 'Hal wants me to go into partnership with him when I get my Ph.D.,' she said. 'He says it's the coming thing, one doctor, one psychologist . . . Without an M.D. I can never give narcosynthesis, shock treatment, a half dozen other things. And he's not at all qualified to give counselling or analysis.'

My frightful evening rose to a climax, burst and sprayed me with cold salt water, slightly muddy. I had never finished high school; here was Olga moving away into the world of doctorates. And having her hand held for guidance by a damned good-looking man, our Hal Levy.

I said: 'I dunno. It seems to me you'd be better off teaming up with some lady doctor if you have to team up with anybody.'

Olga laughed, and stopped pacing. 'If I didn't know you so well,' she said, 'I'd think you were jealous.' A remark which shook my faith in psychologists. 'Why, Hal is quite well-to-do, and there's room in his office for me. It would cost like hell to buy my own setup, besides having to chore around the clinics meeting doctors who'd refer to me. Most M.D.s are inclined to keep the practice inside the A.M.A.'

'You don't have to decide at once,' I said. But she was cutting my heart, liver and lights out with little slashes of a dull knife. We were back to money, and I was almost certain to be unemployed.

'That was a piece of news I was

keeping for you,' Olga said. 'Professor Farber says I can take my viva voce any time now. The paper I did on Patten General will stand up as a thesis, he says.' That was the hospital for the insane where she had worked as an orderly to do research. 'I might get my doctorate in a few weeks.'

She was ten years younger than I, she was still short of her thirtieth birthday by a comfortable margin. She had the education, but I had the experience; her friends from now on might tolerate a successful police officer; they would not go out of their way to be polite to a night watchman.

Most men don't have to face the prospect of losing a job and a wife all in one day. I said: 'Let's go to bed.'

10

Morning was fine and clear; I wasn't. But I put on my best light-weight uniform, complete with solid gold lieutenant's bars. Olga sat quietly by me as I drove her to the bus line she took to the campus. Then she pecked my cheek before she slid out. 'Your strength is as the strength of ten because you've had so much experience in dirty fighting,' she said, and joined the knot of people waiting for the bus. Standing there, she opened one of her textbooks, and was at once lost in it.

Still chuckling, I turned back for the station house — Civic Security Center — and whatever hell had been prepared for me.

Bill Leatherwood was on the switchboard, Drew Lasley at the high reception desk. Like me, he was in the uniform he usually reserved for making speeches and other dress-up occasions. He said: 'Captain Davis is in his office, Andy. After you've read the papers, he wants to see you.'

I must have made a face. Both Leatherwood and Lasley laughed. Bill Leatherwood said: 'Comes the revolution, we won't have newspapers, lieutenant.'

So I went down to my office. Somebody — Leatherwood, probably, acting under Jack Davis's orders — had covered, my desk top, neatly, with the morning press. The Los Angeles papers, and one from the county seat. I sat down and read.

No impulse came to me to get scissors and paste and start a scrapbook for my children, if any. I read that I was more at home guarding ammunition dumps than peaceful suburbs. I had, in direct fashion, made an arrest a few moments after the discovery of Norma Patterson; the wrong arrest, but, apparently content with any arrest, I had called off the hunt for the fugitive.

Said fugitive was still at large. Nobody said so, because there are libel laws, but the reason the rapist was still at large was because I had called off the chase for twenty minutes or so. They implied that by juxtaposition.

A fancy word for a cop to know.

The Naranjo Vista police force had issued almost a thousand traffic tickets in the last year. I hadn't known that; I supposed most of them had been for parking. But it had never before been tested in a major crime.

It —

And I —

And the shooting of Norman Patterson. I was unable to prevent a foul fiend — well, they didn't quite use that one, but almost — from prowling the environs of our peaceful city, but I was quick on the trigger to shoot the already grief-stricken Patterson. The bullet passed within an inch of making him a cripple for life.

This was luck, as I had expected.

Now comes one Bailey Spratt, vice president of the PTA, member of the sheriff's posse, war hero, churchgoer, etc., with an interview. 'The Citizens' Committee of Naranjo Vista, of which I have the honor to be president, is certainly going to look into the way our community is being policed. I am sure that we shall find that many of our officers are just what we always assumed they all were: honest, hard-working men, indifferent to weather conditions or long hours of work or anything else but their proud duty of protecting our lives and property. However, every barrel is liable to have a rotten apple in it; and we are going to leave no stone unturned to root these rotten apples — pray we only find one or two — out and banish them forever from Naranjo Vista.'

Mr. Spratt was also corresponding secretary of the Metaphor Mixers of America, it seemed.

The phone rang. 'Bob Myers to see the lieutenant.'

'Nope.'

Sitting there, I stared at the papers. One thing stood out. They were after me, not Jack Davis. You would hardly know from the press that Naranjo Vista had a chief; I was criminal investigation officer, night chief, and everything else. The papers were using a rifle, not a shotgun.

140

Opening my desk drawer, I took out a sheet of department letterhead. My fountain pen worked at the first touch, which is not its habit. I wrote the date and then Jack Davis's name and title, and then Dear Captain: — and then I wrote my resignation and signed it, big and clear. Five by five, as the radiomen say. Then I blotted it and made an envelope for it and folded it and stood up and walked down the hall to Jack Davis's larger office.

Patrolman Mires was on duty outside the captain's office. I said: 'Tell Captain Davis I'd like to see him.'

Mires looked at me strangely. 'We got orders the office is always open to you, lieutenant.'

'Tell him I'm here, Jimmy.'

So Jimmy Mires hit the switch box and said: 'Lieutenant Bastian to see the captain,' all correct and military.

The squawk box said to send me in. The last thing I saw was Jimmy Mires smiling at me. He was a sort of somber kid, but he managed a pretty good grin.

I'd come a long ways down in the last

few hours, when my own juniors thought they had to encourage me.

To my surprise, Jack Davis was not alone. A small, mean-looking guy of about fifty was sitting at one side of his desk; and my ever-loving pal, Bailey Spratt, was in a straight chair at the front of the desk.

I clicked my heels and saluted like a Marine honor guard hailing an ambassador; I really threw a ball at Jack. He returned the honor without too much embarrassment.

'Grab a chair, Andy, and sit in. This is Mr. Dewitt, he is vice-president of the Bartlett Construction Company. And I think you've met Mr. Spratt.'

'Last night,' I said. 'Good morning, Mr. Spratt.'

Bailey Spratt was in a business suit today. No guns showed through the slick tailoring. Maybe he disarmed to make his living. He said: 'Yeah, I had the pleasure of meeting the lieutenant last night. And I wanta tell you, I was a captain in the Air Force — '

'I'm a major in the Army,' I said, 'but

don't bother to call me sir, Mr. Spratt.'

Jack Davis frowned, Bailey Spratt got red in the face, but little Mr. Dewitt just cleared his throat. He said: 'It is unfortunate that Mr. Bartlett is away just now. I understand you know him personally, Mr. Bastian.'

'Yes,' I said. I did; I knew him and had done favors for him. Mr. Bartlett was not important in Naranjo Vista; he was just the man who had built our five thousand homes. Under the sales contracts, the buyers paid no taxes for the first few years; instead Bartlett Construction — Mr. Bartlett — furnished police, fire and health protection, removed the garbage, flowed water to and sewage away from every house — and paid the bill.

Mr. Bartlett wasn't important at all.

'Last vacation,' Jack Davis said, 'Ralph Bartlett stayed with Andy Bastian and his wife, his father being in Europe.'

Mr. Dewitt said: 'Yes. A great honor. The government has lent Mr. Bartlett to several foreign countries to supervise housing projects.'

Bailey Spratt moved his muscular body

on the uncomfortable chair Jack Davis had assigned him to. He said: 'Yeah, yeah, yeah, and now that we've drunk our pink tea, can we all pull our little fingers in and get down to business?' He slapped a piece of paper lying on Jack's desk. 'I got here a petition, signed by fifty householders of Naranjo Vista — and not one of them in arrears on his payments, Mr. Dewitt — asking for Lieutenant Bastian's resignation.'

Mr. Dewitt said: 'Mr. Bartlett — ' and let it trail away.

Mr. Dewitt had a sort of milky way of talking, but his eyes were like a raccoon's, and when he shut his mouth his little chin jutted out a good inch from his thin lips. He was Mr. Bartlett's vice president, and while I had very little respect for Mr. Bartlett as a father — Ralph, of whom Olga and I were very fond, had had a rough time — when it came to business, Sidney Bartlett didn't throw money away on yes-men for vice presidents.

Bailey Spratt said: 'Mr. Bartlett is just like any other man in business. We're customers, and the customer has gotta be right, or you go out of business.'

My memory is well trained. I said: 'You sell cars, don't you, Mr. Spratt?'

He glared. 'I have a factory agency, mister.' He named the make of car.

'This department uses four of your cars,' I said. 'The county has over a hundred of them. Other cooperating police departments use them, too. In other words, captain, we're customers.'

'Listen, mister, if you're trying to threaten me, knock it off.'

Up till now I had been relaxing in the chair Jack Davis had waved me to. Now I stood up and looked down at Bailey Spratt. 'I was trying to threaten you, yes. But just to show you how it feels to be threatened. Mr. Dewitt here doesn't have to listen to your loud-mouthing. You've bought the houses, and if you want to sell them, that's your business. Captain Davis doesn't have to listen to you. He hired me, and on my record that was a good thing to do. Last night I goofed, I fluffed, and badly, and that is no good.' I reached in my pocket. 'Captain, here is my resignation. You'll notice that it reads for the good of the department. You'll also notice that it was written before I knew that Householder Spratt was here.'

'You're a hell of a soldier,' Bailey Spratt said. 'Quitting under fire.'

'You can't have it both ways,' I said. 'Spratt, were you a pilot, or what?'

'I was a supply officer,' Bailey Spratt said.

'That is what I thought.'

Jack Davis slapped his desk. 'Cut it out,' he said. 'You're squabbling like a couple of kids.' He reached out. 'Ever play three card poker? It's called Spanish monte. Takes three cards. Now, let's see. We got your card, Mr. Spratt, this petition. We got your card, Andy, your resignation. I got a card, too, and I don't know but what it takes the hand.'

He slid open the center drawer of the desk, took out a sheet of legal-sized paper. It had no printed heading.

'Let me read it,' Captain Jack Davis said. ' "We, the undersigned officers of the Naranjo Vista Police Department hereby tender our resignations, to take force — ' that's kind of a strange way of putting it,

146

but I didn't write this — 'when and if Lieutenant Andrew Bastian is removed from our department, by resignation or dismissal.' It's signed by every member of the department. The last signature is that of Jack E. Davis, which means me.'

Bailey Spratt beat the desk again with the flat of his hand. 'That's illegal,' he said. 'Police officers can't quit and leave a community without protection. I'm a pretty big man in politics around here, and I'm taking this right to the district attorney.'

Mr. Dewitt said: 'Mr. Spratt, you may be big in politics, but it seems to me that you have just lost the votes of the entire police department.' His bright eyes didn't twinkle, his thin lips didn't quirk; I couldn't tell if he thought he was being funny or not. Me, I thought he was a riot, somewhat better than the Marx Brothers; but then I was prejudiced. Mr. Dewitt let what he'd said sink in, and then reached in his own inside pocket. 'I have never indulged in card games, Captain Davis, nor, I might add, in any other form of gaming, but if there is a game involving four cards, we are, perhaps, playing it. I have here a telegram from Mr. Bartlett, and I read: 'Tell Andy Bastian I'm behind him all the way. Don't bother me with details. Signed, Sidney Bartlett.' Message ends.'

Bailey Spratt stood up. 'By God, you haven't heard the last of this.' He marched out.

Mr. Dewitt said: 'He has been trying to sell Bartlett Construction a line of trucks. I must say, he's not the sort of salesman I'd hire.'

Mr. Dewitt stood up. He held out his hand to me, and I shook it; it was like holding a five-year-old pine cone.

Then he shook hands with Jack Davis, and then my chief and I were alone.

'All very pretty,' I said. 'What it means is, you'd better not use my resignation for a couple of weeks, till you can make it look like you didn't crack under pressure.'

Jack Davis said: 'Don't be a damned fool, Andy. There's a hell of a lot of work to do around here. Who's going to do it if you loaf around my office all day?'

So I marched back to my office. Every

damn cop I passed in the hail felt he had to salute me, and since I was in uniform, I had no choice but to snap the ball back to them. If this went on, the Naranjo Vista force would be so exhausted from saluting that it wouldn't have energy to do anything else.

I latched my office door and changed into the flannel slacks and tweed coat I kept in my closet.

But I'd be a liar if I didn't say that I felt pretty good.

11

There was routine stuff on my desk — duty rolls to initial, a letter from an insurance company to answer about a break-and-entry, and so on. It was an hour before I got it cleared away, and then I leaned back and told the switchboard to get me the lab at county.

After a while a voice said: 'Lab, Lieutenant Miller.'

'Lieutenant Bastian at Naranjo Vista. I don't suppose Sergeant Ernen is there, but I'd like to know how far along he is on the profile of our rapist.'

Miller laughed. 'Ernie's here all right,' he said. 'I don't know when that guy sleeps. I can put him on, but I've been looking over his work, and I think it would be smart if you came up here.'

I took a department car, a marked one. For a while I would have to be very careful what vehicle I drove where; Bailey Spratt could be out to nail me if I drove a

150

city car to lunch, for instance. Hence, the car with the shield on the side, though I was in plainclothes myself; to use a plain car might look like sneaking.

We were having lovely weather. The benevolent state of California had the sprinklers going on both sides of the freeway; they made little rainbows as they played down on the iceplant and the lantanas and the semi-tropical pampas grass that held down the soil of the cutbanks.

Olga would never let me water our garden when the full sun was out; she said that the little drops of water would make burning glasses on the leaves, and scorch them.

The State Highway Department was obviously not married to Olga.

Poor C.H.D.; I was luckier than they.

But would I be luckier in a few months when Olga got her Ph.D. and moved into practice as a clinical psychologist? It was already bad enough at the parties we went to; young executives, young dentists, young scientists and their wives were ill-at-ease with a police officer.

The same people would be just as uneasy with head shrinkers and soul divers as they were with me. So we'd move in different circles, and they'd be tough ones for me to turn in, me with my USAFI high school certificate and my profound knowledge of greed and misery, violence and despair.

Seeing myself, in my mind's eye, at those parties, I had a horrid thought; they wouldn't laugh at me because I would have a gun bulking under my clothes, and nobody laughs at the man with the gun.

And there, in the bright sunlight, driving the well-serviced department car through traffic that deferred to the shield and the red light, I uttered a little, almost invisible prayer; me, who has never been religious because the cheesewits and hypocrites who ran the Boys' Home had tried to force me into religion.

This was my prayer: Dear God, don't let my gun rob my brains. Amen.

The sign for the Civic Center turnoff brought me back to business. I got out of the fast lane into the right hand one without much difficulty because I was driving a police car; California freeways do not give way for civilians very readily.

Once I got off the freeway, traffic thinned down and driving was actually easier. In two or three minutes I was in the parking lot behind the new ten-story Civic Center.

There were coin-in-the-slot parking spaces, and then there were free ones reserved for police cars; I took one of the latter, though I was out of my jurisdiction.

A girl was typing some kind of report at the desk opposite the elevator on the third, or lab, floor. She looked like civilian personnel. We didn't run to such luxuries in our little department; our sworn officers did their own typing. She told me where I could find Sergeant Ernen.

He was there all right, hunched over a Bunsen burner, blowing through a pipe to make the flame melt some kind of metal into a bead. He cocked an eyebrow at me, and I perched on one of the high stools and waited for him.

He quit whatever he was doing, and pointed at the bead. 'Not your case, Andy.

Somebody's been making slugs and selling them for the parking meters. Not counterfeiting, did you know that? I'm trying to find out what the alloy is, might tell us where he's buying his metal. I think it's pot metal from a linotype machine, but I'm not sure yet.'

He stood up, stretched, and popped a cigarette into his mouth, lit it with a wooden match rasped against his thumb-nail; there was a deep black notch on the nail from the habit. 'Come along, the loot wants to sit in on this.'

So we went into another office, and I met Lieutenant Miller, who was wearing a white smock, like a mad scientist in a movie, if they still make that kind of movie. Hands got shook, I got a chair, Miller and I lit cigarettes to match the one Ernie had already gulped halfway down.

The sarge leaned back. 'I don't have to tell you two that there's two kinds of evidence: the kind we can believe in ourselves, and not bring into court, and the kind that's legal evidence. Wanta hear it?'

Lieutenant Miller said of course we did.

Ernie shook his dogged little head. 'You understand, in a case of this kind, if some cop goes on what I'm saying and makes a pinch, he's liable to end up with a false arrest charge. So okay. Our guy is in his late thirties, early forties. That I make from the condition of his hair; it's not gray, but the pigment count is way down. Not heavy, but a stocky kind of fellow. He was dressed in tropical worsted suntans, not GI but like the kind an officer, Army or maybe Air Force or even Navy might buy for himself. I mean, if it was Air Force or Navy, the officer'd be a couple of shades off regulation, but for wearing on leave or into town or to the Officers' Club — whoever called an officer down for a couple of shades?'

'Men who used to be officers give their uniforms away when they wear out at the knees,' I said. 'I mean, we use them for gardening, or even as summer slacks, but there's plenty of expensive cloth left when the pants get to the Goodwill or the Salvation Army.'

Ernie nodded. 'Yeah, sure. And I didn't get enough cloth to decide if it was clean, or greasy and sweat-stained. You got it in mind that a bum did this.'

'I got it in mind,' I said. 'It's a bum's kind of crime. Rape in an open field.'

Lieutenant Miller put out his cigarette and fished a pipe out of a desk drawer. Southern California makes actors of them all; the time had come for deep thought, and deep thought required a pipe for a prop. He got the pipe going, and said: 'Not always, Lieutenant Bastian. I mean, not only bums rape. Though, with money, it isn't hard to get any kind of tail you want, in these times, in this county. But, take Ernie's man, and for a minute let's pretend he is, if not rich, at least getting along. In two ways; he's getting along in years, too, ending his thirties, starting his forties . . . Like all of us here,' Miller said.

I stared at him. Ernie fidgeted in his chair. Miller raised the pipe by its bowl, and waved it at us. 'You've been a young man of promise. All of a sudden you realize you're not going to be young ever again. Your wife no longer admires you; she loves you, you're in the habit of each other, but she knows you for what you are, and, hell, who of us can stand that kind of examination?' He laughed. 'I can't. So there's a young girl — nineteen, Ernie? — and she waves it in your face every time she sees you. There's one in every neighborhood. And because she's young, you think how it would be with her — I don't mean how she'd feel, which would be good, but how she doesn't know enough to know you're bluffing your way through life, you aren't half as wonderful as you thought you were going to be when you were nineteen. And then, of course, you find she's just having fun with you, practicing on you, making sport of your thinning hair. So, one night — '

He made a sweeping gesture with the pipe and popped it into his mouth. Me, I was thinking how different this talk was from what Olga's white collar friends must imagine cop talk to be like.

Ernie said: 'Hell, Bill, I got a million things to do in the lab. Lemme finish, and then you two brains put it together. I'm just a technician.'

'I still favor the bum theory.'

Ernie said: 'Andy, I don't think so. In my opinion, the guy was wearing some expensive kind of clothes, good tropical worsted, and it was his own, not a hand-me-down. Second, he had expensive bridgework. So I'm afraid your bum is out, Andy.'

Now it was Lieutenant Bill Miller's turn to get excited.

'Bridgework? Great grief, Ernie, that's the finest kind of clue. Why, stiffs we pick up along the highway, we'd never identify a third of them without bridgework.'

Ernie looked out the window of his boss's office. You could see him thinking that if everybody did his police work as neatly as a lab technician, life would be a lovely thing. He said: 'Take it easy, loot. I don't mean this guy took his plate outa his mouth while he knocked off a piece, and then went away and forgot it. I mean the girl got her fingers in his mouth while they were struggling, and he bit down on them. I looked in on her last night, in County Hospital. She was

158

still knocked out.'

He put three fingers in his own mouth and came down on them gently, to show us. Then he held them out, shiny with saliva. Tooth marks were visible, but they faded while we watched. 'Of course, he gave them a hell of a harder bite than that, but it isn't like a bite in the fleshy side of the palm. Now, once, I got one of those — '

Ernie broke off before he could violate his own sense of neatness by reminiscing. 'There's good dental work,' he said, 'and there's cheap stuff, like a wino might get done in a clinic. I'm not getting up before some smart lawyer and saying this was an expensive job, but I'm willing to tell you lads that I think it was. Cheap teeth are all the same — China clippers. Good ones are a little irregular, to make 'em look real. But they don't bite like real, as you know if you got a bridge.'

Bill Miller smiled at me. 'Your bum theory is going out the window of Ernie's lab, Andy,' he said, cheerfully. It was the first time he'd called me by my first name.

Ernie stood up. 'There's more, but it's pretty positive stuff, you got it in writing. Five feet eight to five feet nine. A hundred and fifty to sixty pounds.' He started for the door. 'I got a million things to do; that lab never catches up. I could use three more technicians, Bill.'

And he was gone.

Bill Miller picked up a typed report from the desk, peeled a carbon off and handed it to me. Except for the hair, there was nothing on it Ernie had given in his confidential report. It mentioned the teeth marks, but not that they had been made by artificial teeth.

Miller said: 'Were there any military meetings in Naranjo Vista that night? Reserve officers of Guard, or something like that? Ernie seemed to favor a uniform.'

'Sheriff's posse?'

The words hung in the air between us. Bill Miller was a Sheriffs Lieutenant of Deputies; like all officers in unincorporated territory, I was a sworn deputy myself.

The posse consisted of everybody who

160

liked that sort of thing and who could help the sheriff get re-elected. Rich men, influential men. Men who could afford tailored uniforms and silver saddles and palominos and pearl-handled guns so they could march in a parade once in a while.

Bill Miller said: 'Ernie is damned good, by the way. I'm supposed to be in charge of all laboratory work, but Ernie really runs the lab. What I do is keep small-time police chiefs off his neck, and politicos; he's not the most tactful guy in the world. He likes you, for some reason.'

'Thanks.'

'I mean, he seldom likes anything big enough to be seen without a microscope.'

Lieutenant Bill Miller glanced out his window at the police parking lot, and smoothed the bowl of his cold pipe with a calloused thumb. 'What Ernie tells you, you can usually act on. I don't think I have to tell you that. If he didn't like you, we wouldn't have passed all this stuff on to you — just the usual report, unidentifiable tooth marks, wool fibers of such and such a grade, not

Ernie's conclusions.'

Standing up, I said: 'The conclusions are my own, the lab work is credited to you.'

'Well, Ernie did say that you collected better specimens for him than he usually gets . . . It sounds like a big shot, doesn't it?'

'A very big shot.'

'But big shots don't commit rape. Despite all that nonsense I gave you about guys of forty. Girl next door to me. I've got a radio shack on my garage roof. Every time I'm up there, she gets in her garden in a bikini to sunbathe. But I haven't raped her, have I?'

'That I wouldn't know,' I said. 'My jurisdiction is just Naranjo Vista, so the squeal wouldn't come to me.'

He looked at me for the space of a full second, and then burst into laughter. Standing up, he put his hand out.

'Nice to meet you, Andy. Next time your business brings you up here, let's eat lunch. You interested in radio?' When I shook my head, he said: 'It's my hobby. Damned interesting.'

'Should think you'd be running communications instead of lab.'

His thumb threw all that out the window. 'Repairman stuff. What I have is like a little Jodrell Banks; missile tracking, and analyzing cosmic rays.'

Before I left his office, I called County General. Nora Patterson was still under sedation; the County had a detective standing by to question her when the doctor said it was all right.

Norman Patterson was resting comfortably, the desk in the prison ward said, and the wino, who had called himself John Davis, had made a legal phone call — out of town, collect — and was now dallying with the idea of the DTs.

No money in going over there to question any of them.

Driving back along the freeway, I thought how little most people knew about cops. Sergeant Ernen, with his test tubes and his reactors, or Lieutenant Miller, with his analysis of cosmic rays, didn't fit the picture of the old-fashioned bull with a rubber hose and a gun butt and a pair of flat feet.

Then I thought of several officers I knew who socked first and asked questions afterwards, and of many more, who had no curiosity at all, and no interests outside their jobs except maybe football and horse racing. These were in the great majority, and they made, in and out, the best cops. Ernen and Miller would never rise above lieutenant; the scientific mind was not rough enough to command a precinct or even a detective squad.

But the sun was still shining on Southern California, and the wind was in the wrong direction to bring us smog from Fontana or Los Angeles, our two big sources. A very nice day, and the case was coming along. Like Bill Miller, I didn't doubt Ernie's analysis. It was no passing bum that had raped Norma Patterson.

Shooting in and out of traffic, making good time back to Naranjo Vista, I thought: neither is it necessarily a big shot. Ernie had jumped to a very old-fashioned conclusion.

Nowadays, factory hands make enough

to buy the best woolen slacks and shirts; filling station boys can afford the best.

I came to the turn-off for Naranjo Vista and then there was three miles through poinsettia fields to the town itself. Obeying all traffic signals, I was going thirty when I hit our model village.

I slowed down some more, and made my decision. Instead of parking in front of the station, I pulled up at the other end of the Community Center, where two of our four doctors had their offices.

Their joint receptionist was a middle-aged lady with artificially whitened hair. She wore a flowered dress instead of a nurse's uniform; psychology to put the patients at their ease?

Dr. Levy had a patient in with him, and would be tied up awhile. Dr. Crossen ought to be free in a moment.

Two dames restraining kids glared at me as I went into Dr. Crossen's office ahead of them. The good doctor was about five years younger than I, in his early thirties, and neat looking in his high-buttoned white jacket. He was standing alongside his desk when I came in. 'What can I do for you, lieutenant?'

'You got the bulletin about reporting a man with a scratched face to us?'

'Yes, yes. And I can assure you I'll be glad to cooperate, but really, I am a pediatrician. None of my patients has grown a beard yet.'

His tone of obvious superiority gave me an ache. Twenty-odd years of training helped me to keep said ache to myself. 'No, you're hardly my man. But doctors cross the lines of their specialities, and doctors get confidences.'

'Which they keep to themselves, officer,' he said, deliberately demoting me.

'I'm looking for a guy with a badly frustrated sex life, doctor.'

As soon as I'd said it, I knew I was making a fool out of myself. I stood and let his amusement claw at me.

'Look wide, lieutenant,' he said, 'and look close. Whose sex life is not frustrated, in our little semi-tropical paradise? Why, it is the trademark of our community, sir, the stigma of our times. The sorts of jobs our neighbors do lead to frustration in all departments, including that of the bed.'

'I suppose so,' I said. 'Examining kids for diaper rash all day would leave me kind of pent up, I imagine.'

So much for twenty-odd years of training. I left him knowing I'd lost the encounter; he'd kept his temper and his cool superiority; I'd lost mine.

Outside, the receptionist said: 'You can go in now, Mrs. Spratt,' and then told me that Dr. Levy was free.

But I was staring at the door closing on Dr. Crossen's office. 'That Mrs. Bailey Spratt?'

The receptionist nodded. 'Yes, and little Dwight.'

I should have paid more attention. All I remembered was a dame like any other thirty-odd-year-old dame; neither very good looking nor very ugly; neither well-dressed nor a slob. With a kid, two years or five years or three months old. Little Dwight. I wondered if Bailey Spratt had named his offspring after Eisenhower . . . I should have been more attentive. I should have given her the well-known smile. Her husband was out to get me, and a little softening on the distaff side would have been politically useful.

All, to hell with politics. I had been brought up to do my job, and leave the rest to my superiors. But now I only had one superior, Jack Davis and he was my friend.

Anything I did reflected on him. I had no right to lose my temper, no right to make enemies; I owed it to Jack not to.

An old woman, at least seventy, came out of Hal Levy's office. People that age were a rarity in Naranjo Vista. She smiled at the receptionist and left, and I was told to go in.

Hal Levy and a girl in a nurse's uniform were drinking coffee together; he was sitting on his desk, she in the doctor's chair. Hal waved his cup at me, and said: 'Hi, Andy. You know Priscilla Hanford, don't you?'

I shook my head. 'My loss.'

'A gallant cop,' Miss Hanford said. 'I'll get you a cup of coffee, Mr. Bastian.'

She went into the next room with a swish of starched white skirts above very good legs. The sight of her cheered me up considerably; she was very good looking, and Hal's relationship with her seemed informal, to say the least. Maybe I was nuts to be jealous of his friendship with Olga.

'You can certainly pick nurses, Hal.'

'Oh, Priss isn't a nurse. They take some sort of course in being office assistants. How to say: 'Doctor is out, why don't you take two aspirins and I'll have him call you when he gets in.''

I laughed. From the open door, Priscilla Hanford said: 'You look like a black coffee man, Mr. Bastian. Right?'

'Lay off, Priss,' Hal said. 'Andy's happily married. You sick, Andy, or just social?'

'Neither,' I said. 'Police business in a half — ' I looked at Priscilla and changed what I was going to say: 'Half-hearted way. We have reasons to believe — I can give it to you, but it's technical, and maybe dull — that the man who raped that girl last night was someone of possible importance and standing here in Naranjo Vista. It changes the whole case.'

Priscilla Hanford sat down and crossed her legs. I looked, and went on: 'Up till now, we've been counting on a Skid Row pickup to break the case. Of course, the L.A. cops and the county men will continue searching along those lines. But I think we're going to find our man right here in Naranjo Vista.'

Hal Levy whistled gently. Priss Hanford uncrossed her legs and bent forward to look at me.

'Which means,' I said, 'that there's a good chance that somebody with a scratched face will come to one of the four doctors here to be treated.'

Hal shook his head. 'People treat their own colds and scratches these days. You would do better to alert the drug stores.'

Priss Hanford said: 'There's a heavy make-up that will cover that sort of thing. A man buying it might be a hot clue.'

'We know a little more about him,' I said. 'Five feet eight, about. Hair light brown, beard darker. Belongs, probably, to one of the reserve units that wears suntans, to the posse or to the gun club.'

Hal Levy fished a cigarette out of his

shirt pocket. Unlike Dr. Crossen, he was in a business suit, not a white outfit. He said: 'I wouldn't care to make you mad at me, Andy. Bailey Spratt has a bruise, not a scratch.'

'You mentioned his name, not I.'

The phone rang. Priss Hanford went to the desk and picked up the receiver. 'Dr. Levy's office . . . Oh, certainly.' She hung up. 'Dr. Crossen wants me to help him a minute.'

When the door had closed behind her, I said: 'That's one hell of a good looking gal you have there, Hal.'

He shrugged. 'Why not? I've got to look at her all day. When she isn't helping out Crossen. His practice isn't big enough to pay for an assistant yet.'

'He's got a damned poor bedside manner.'

Hal Levy laughed. 'You cross night-sticks with Crossen? He doesn't like cops. Something when he was an intern, I don't know what.'

I stood up. 'Bring Priss to dinner some night.'

Hal frowned. 'I don't know. It's

supposed to be a bad idea to mingle with your help. But she looks like she'd make such nice mingling, I'm weakening . . . Andy, has Olga told you what we've been talking about?'

'You mean, going into partnership?' All of a sudden I was tired of horsing around. 'That's one reason I've been pushing you at Miss Hanford.'

His laughter was deep and rich and natural. 'Jealous, pal? Maybe ten years from now, but at the moment Olga's the most in-love girl I know. I'll admit I've regretted it, a time or two. Yes, I offered her a partnership when she gets her Ph.D. But, frankly, I've also told her she's a fool not to go on and get her M.D., too. With the courses she's already taken, she could knock it off in three years.'

My heart rose. For three years, maybe four, Olga would remain a student; she would not make that terrific jump in status over me. In three years, or four, I might rise in status myself, though I didn't see how.

A daydream started. I would take courses in theoretical criminology, and with what I knew about the practical side, get to be a professor at the university. Three years was a breathing spell.

'What's Olga's objection to that?' I asked. 'She hasn't mentioned it to me at all.'

'She doesn't want to be a burden on you all that time. Wants to start earning money.'

'She's nuts. I'm making plenty for both.' Hell, I got a good salary, and I got half pay from the Army as a major; three hundred and sixty-five bucks every month. You never know your own wife, I thought; Olga's worried about money.

'We'll talk it over,' I said, and left. Hal Levy and I knew each other well enough not to bother with the shaking of hands.

Now I had a new worry. Olga was shaky about my earning capacity. She thought I might get fired. It was the only thing that could worry her, because we never spent what I made anyway; we put a little away every month . . .

Hal would speak to Crossen. I could send a sergeant to the drug store, and go see the other two doctors later. I had better get to the station. Sergeant Hahn was on the desk. Before I even had a chance to sign the blotter, he said: 'Squeal over at the high school. Captain Davis is there, he said to send you the minute you showed, sir.'

So back down to the garage and the department car. Less than a minute to the high school; park the car, check the gun to be sure it's loose in the holster, up the steps, into the place. I knew where the office was now.

A little girl, a student, was receiving in the principal's suite. I said: 'I'm Lieutenant Bastian. Captain Davis wanted me here.'

Her eyes were wide with excitement. 'The chief's in the principal's office with Miss Crowther.'

I went in. Eleanor Crowther and Jack Davis were there; so was our Fire Chief, Dave Simpson. So was the principal's desk, or a desk, or what was left of a desk. Fire had gutted it out; there was a pile of charred wood standing on the concrete floor. The carpet was ruined. Wall-to-wall, too bad. Dave looked around, said: 'Oh,

Andy. Come and look.'

I went and looked. Then I said: 'Arson?'

Dave Simpson was sure. 'Arson is the burning of a dwelling in the night time. This was maybe deliberate, yes, but not arson.'

Eleanor Crowther had her hands together, twisting a wisp of handkerchief. It was going to tear in a minute.

'I've seen this before,' she said. 'At a city school. It's — it's a very bad symptom.'

She had helped me the night before, under somewhat grueling conditions. She had reported for work this morning, when she probably should have rested. I softened my voice as much as possible, and said: 'Symptom of what, Miss Crowther?'

'Malcontent,' she said. 'Disrest.' I suppose she meant unrest. Her voice was very high. 'The kids — oh, the kids are about to break loose. It started before by burning the principal's desk, just like this. And then the library . . . '

Dave Simpson said: 'I'll post a

watchman in the library. And one outside in the files. This is a fireproof building.'

Jack Davis asked: 'Is there really a genuine fireproof building?'

Dave Simpson said: 'No.'

I was wondering if we could call on Sergeant Ernen to come down and look at this mess. Some of the ashes were papers; I wasn't a good enough lab man to take latent fingerproofs off paper ashes, but Ernie probably was.

Jack Davis said: 'Trouble with a school case like this, if you catch your culprit, it's just juvenile delinquency and a suspended sentence. They ought to make whipping legal.'

I looked at him in amazement. He sounded like one of those sheriff's posse amateurs, with his brain in his holster. I said: 'These are citizens and the children of taxpayers, not a bunch of POWs.' We had met in a prison stockade, guarding Afrika Korpsmen. We'd both been sergeants, then, and we considered ourselves tough; but every time we had to go up to the line, out in the desert, to bring back some more of those sour krauts — as we called them — Jack went to the chaplain and prayed awhile. Not being religious, I had just hoped.

'Coming when Mr. Adams is not here,' Miss Crowther said, 'I just don't know what to do.'

So Walt Adams was still laid up. Bailey Spratt apparently carried quite a wallop, for a gun crank. I said: 'Is there a pay booth or a direct wire around? I want to call Walt's doctor, and I'd as soon it didn't go through the school switchboard.'

Miss Crowther said: 'I already called Dr. Levy. He won't permit Mr. Adams to leave his bed. He says there's danger of a fractured bone, and concussion.'

Funny that Hal Levy hadn't mentioned it a few minutes ago. He knew I was a close friend of Walt's. But then, thinking it over, it wasn't funny at all. Doctors' ethics. Never tell an outsider anything.

Well police ethics were the same; there was stuff it would have been unethical for me to tell Olga. To me, doctors were just another brand of civilian.

'When you're acting principal, Miss

Crowther, who is assistant acting principal?'

She looked puzzled. 'I don't know. It's never come up.'

'It's up now. How about your gym teacher?'

'Mr. Eldrey?'

'If that's his name,' I said. She was going cheesewit on me. We weren't going to get anywhere till I got her out of there and under a doctor's care. I said: 'He a good man?'

'Oh, yes, I'm sure . . . '

Jack Davis was looking at me gratefully as I took over. I opened the door, told the student secretary to ask Mr. Eldrey to come to the office, and went back. 'Miss Crowther, who's been in here this morning?'

'Oh, dozens of people,' she said. 'Students for this and that, the janitor, me to get some of Mr. Adams' papers. I've been in here and out again and — '

'One other question. Is Dr. Levy your physician?'

'Why, no. Dr. Barnhart.'

I looked at Jack Davis, for permission

to go hunt a phone. Of course, the one that had been on Walt Adams's desk was ruined; a mess of melted plastic and gaping wires. It was possible that it had loused up the whole local exchange, shorting out in the fire.

Jack didn't give me the nod to go. Instead he walked gravely out of the office. My chief was giving a good imitation of a broken reed.

Miss Crowther watched him go, incuriously. Then she walked over to me on her high heels, and took my arm in her two hands. 'Lieutenant Bastian, you're very strong aren't you?' Since she was kneading my biceps, the question sounded as though she wanted me to move furniture, but I guess she was referring to my moral stamina. 'You are going to stop this, aren't you?'

'Miss Crowther, you're in safe hands.' To be doing something, I turned to Dave Simpson, bright and blue and gold in his fire chiefs uniform. 'What would burn a desk like this?'

'Walt Adams kept a big can of lighter fluid in his desk. It probably got hot from burning paper, exploded, and — wow!'

'Yeah. Wow.' This time when I tramped to the door, Miss Crowther went along. I could feel her fingernails through the wool of my sports jacket. I said to the kid outside: 'You call Mr. Eldrey?'

She nodded, and then saw Miss Crowther over my shoulder. 'Oh, Miss Crowther, Nora and I always go to the cafeteria around this time. Could I?'

I said: 'Nope. No, sit tight for a few minutes. And get those people I asked you for.'

She said: 'But Nora Patterson and I — ' Then she remembered what had happened to Norma, and shut up.

I stared at her. Glowering eyes told me I had made a teen-age enemy. Very alarming, very frightening. According to current literature, I should get under a bed someplace and cower.

But the kid was bursting with information, and I didn't want her spraying it around the school cafeteria and starting a panic. Anyway, she was chubby enough; she didn't need any milk.

I ought to swear her in as a junior

officer. But I had left my mail-order G-man kit at home in the toy closet. I towed Miss Crowther back to the center of the room, and then decided to sit on the leather couch; it had been far enough away from the desk to be unscorched.

But when I sat down, Miss Crowther sat down, too, still holding onto my arm; and now she lowered her head to rest on my shoulder.

Jack Davis chose that moment to come back in.

'Dr. Barnhart's up in the city,' he said. 'His office nurse said to take Miss Crowther home and put her to bed. She's got some sedative pills on prescription, and it's all right to give her two. I tried to get Miss Hellman, but she's tied up. You've got the duty, Andy.'

'Jack — '

'I'm chief,' he said, happily. 'You gotta do what I tell you. Anyway, the lady seems more at home with you than with me.'

'She's in lousy shape,' I said. I was aware that we were talking about Miss Crowther as though she wasn't there, but

181

she didn't seem to mind, or even to know it.

I said: 'I've got a rape case on my hands.'

'You've got more than that,' Jack Davis said. 'Los Angeles got a make on little John Davis — ' he grimaced, 'on his fingerprints. His real name is Wright, thank God. Next of kin is a father up the coast; he'll be arriving today. I want you to talk to him. I'm damned glad I'm chief,' Jack Davis said. 'And to think, I got it by getting out of the Army two years before you did, even if you were my superior.'

'Very funny. Funny indeed.'

He said: 'Truth is, I'd better hang around my office. Drew Lasley's going to sock one of those posse men pretty soon.'

'Bailey Spratt?'

'He's the worst. There are others. By the way, the one you climbed, Joe Harg, resigned from the posse; you must have made him see the light.'

'Maybe I ought to be an evangelist.'

Jack smiled. I was sitting on the couch, with Miss Crowther hanging onto my arm; Jack was leaning against the wall; Dave Simpson was poking around the burnt desk.

Jack Davis said: 'If we could hang those three break-and-entries on somebody, there'd be less posse heat.'

I nodded. I'd forgotten them. They had started the whole amateur police trouble, but I had forgotten them.

I said, vaguely: 'I checked it to Juvenile Probation. Just kid stuff.'

Dave Simpson misunderstood me. He looked up from the desk, and said: 'Yeah. Time was, I remember, when they sent bulletins marked secret around to the fire stations, about thermite, and what it was and how it could burn through concrete. Now, any kid who's in a science club knows, and over at the malt shop where they all go, there's probably a couple of comic books telling you all about it. Sometimes I wonder if all this education is a good thing. Thank God, they didn't use thermite on this job.'

He was making a joke, and he and Jack Davis laughed. And then, after a minute, I felt like laughing, too, because I remembered Miss Bridge and what she had said about the Spratt case and the other burglaries. I had just broken them. I said: 'See you in a few minutes,' and went outside, still laughing, though I was about to break a minor law or two.

It was a slight trick of memory to remember the other two names, besides Spratt, on the complaint sheets. Stern and Thorne. I asked the student clerk if she would get the Stern kid and the Thorne kid and the Spratt kid up to the office. 'Both Thorne boys, and Elaine Stern, too?'

'Just the boys,' I said, 'and then you can take your coffee break.'

'Milk,' she said. 'Nora and I always drink a bottle of milk and eat a piece of fruit in the middle of the morning. For our complexions.'

'Okay.'

'They're all in 10-B,' she said. 'I could stop and send them up on the way to the cafeteria.'

'Okay.'

She went out, swishing slightly, for

practice. I sat on the edge of her desk and tried a cigarette; my throat was dry and it didn't taste right. Jack Davis stuck his head out of the inner office and said: 'Hey, Andy, your lady friend is getting the screaming meemies.'

'Really?'

'No, just the muttering kind so far. How about getting her out of here?'

'In a minute. I'm imitating a detective. Get out of here. This is illegal.'

The boys arrived in a group, all four of them. Young Spratt was not as round faced as his father, but twenty years of rich food would heighten the resemblance. The others looked like boys; the only interesting thing about them was that the Thorne boys, though they were in the same class, were a foot different in height. I asked them if they were twins.

The shorter one said: 'We're not even related.'

'Oh. Which one of you lives on Coronado Lane?'

Big one did. I sent the little one back to class. I yawned, and puffed on my nasty tasting cigarette. I said: 'I'm Lieutenant

185

Bastian, police. All three of you guys had break-ins at your houses. Which of you did it?'

Six young eyes looked back at me with the innocent expression of a dairy cow. A six-eyed dairy cow.

I shrugged, and blew smoke at them. 'Okay, men, now we take a walk. We go down to the police station, and we line you up, and we bring in the man who runs the malt shop here by the school, and we ask him which of you suddenly had a lot of extra money. Let's see, there was liquor taken, too. We find out if any of you missed school from being sick. We call that a hangover.'

Then I acted like they weren't there. I blew smoke at the ceiling. I let my coat slide back to show the gun in its clamshell holster. In other words, I acted. Like a dick on TV.

Finally the Thorne boy broke it. 'We didn't have anything to do with it.'

That was all I needed. I said: 'We? How come you can speak for anybody but yourself? You guys call yourselves the Three Musketeers or something?'

And they all got red in the face. Oh, I am a smart cop; I can outthink Class 10-B any day in the week. I sat down at the typewriter, typed: 'We, the under-signed, robbed our parents' houses and made it look like someone had done it from outside,' and handed it to them.

There was damned little palaver before they signed. I shooed them back to class, and went back to the sooty inner room. I handed Jack Davis the sheet. 'You take care of this, captain.'

He looked at it and gaped. 'How did you get this?'

'Illegally,' I said. 'You'd better not ask. By the way, Probation calls these cases S & H, for Son and Heir.'

He grinned, uncertainly. It really wasn't much of a document; but maybe he could use it to keep Bailey Spratt quiet. I doubted it; all it would do was bring a charge of malfeasance against me. But at least Jack Davis would get off my neck about the break-and-entries.

Miss Crowther had hold of my arm again. I said: 'Let's go. I'm taking you home.'

Dave Simpson laughed. 'Cops have all the fun. Us firemen, just once in a while, have to break down a bathroom door that gets stuck. I'm on my way, Andy. I'll notify the insurance company that covers municipal property; they'll have investigators here in no time.'

'I'm checking it to them,' I said. 'If you see any reporters, tell them the police have decided it definitely is an accident. We haven't, but it will keep the Vista calmed down while we all work.'

'A good idea,' Dave said. He made his goodbyes, and started out. At the door he passed the gym teacher, Mr. Eldrey. I told him he was acting principal; he took one look at Eleanor Crowther and nodded, silently. For once I had run into a strong, silent guy; maybe my luck was turning. He just went into the outer office and phoned the custodian to move a desk up into the principal's office. He and Jack Davis could handle what had to be handled.

12

Broad daylight in Naranjo Vista, and me driving along with a lady slumped over on my shoulder. No grief, no danger; Olga and jealousy had never met except in a case history about someone else.

Miss Crowther was out like a lady after a three-day drunk. Her cheeks tried to bore through the cloth of my coat, and her lips mumbled nonsense syllables. I knew where she lived; I drove towards there at a decent, legal pace.

No danger, and I had been right — no grief; and I had been wrong. Our automatic traffic equipment turned the light to red, and I stopped in the right hand lane; before it could turn green, another car pulled up alongside me.

From over a patch of adhesive tape, a hating eye glared at me. My pal, Bailey Spratt.

His voice was harsh. 'A little smooching party, lieutenant? Having a joy ride on the taxpayers' time?'

Temper, Bastian, temper. ''Morning, Mr. Spratt.'

The light changed; I started up. So did he, bearing to the right, pushing me toward the curb. Either I went, or the paint on the car did. Paint cost money; I went.

When my tire hit the curb, I stopped. Bailey Spratt was climbing out of his car; I removed Miss Crowther from my shoulder, leaned her against the right door, reached over to make sure the door was locked, and then got out on my own side.

He was the right height — under five feet ten. He was strong enough to beat a girl into subjection, to trap her while she clawed at his face. He was everything I hated in the world.

And, of course, I knew he hadn't harmed Nora Patterson, that my dreams of hanging the crime on him were fantasy. It would have been a pleasure, but it just wasn't so. Manners.

I said: 'Something I can do for you Mr. Spratt?'

'Yep. You can tell me where you were all morning. I been trying to get you.'

'Why, Mr. Spratt. I've been working. To be specific, I took a trip to the county seat, to the sheriff's building there. On duty.'

His small eyes blinked at me in our strong, healthy sunlight. 'Don't you think I'm not making a call there myself, later today.'

'Mr. Spratt, I'd like to give you a famous old American saying, slightly changed. 'Get there first with the most beefs'.' Then, suddenly, I grinned, and put out my hand. Pure phony, but this was duty, too. 'Let's start all over again. I've really got no beef against you; since you never heard of me before yesterday, you have none against me. Let's stop sniffing around each other like a couple of strange dogs.'

But my selling technique was off. He didn't even look at the hand I held out to him. He said: 'You calling me a dog, copper?'

'You know better than that.'

'You let a filthy rapist get away last

night,' Spratt said. 'You pulled my gang off the streets to show what a big shot you are, and the rat got away. I got a lot of money invested in Naranjo Vista; you knocked some of it off. Houses are not worth much in a town where girls can get beaten and raped.'

That wasn't what he was sore about, of course. It was my running down his honorary deputy's badge, making it look like nothing at all. But I still had a job to do; I couldn't mention that. I couldn't mention the fact that he ran his own home so badly his son robbed it. I said: 'I still want to get along with you, Mr. Spratt. Let me put it this way: You have a business. I have nothing to do but enforce the law. Leave it to me, leave it to the department. If you had a hot prospect for a car sale, you'd hate to drop him and have to go running around the streets, chasing crooks or traffic violators.'

But I'd said the wrong thing; his eyes had lit up. Of course, there was nothing he'd like better than to take a prospect along with him as he went, swinging through the streets at ninety miles an hour, siren open, red light glowing. But the California Highway Patrol wouldn't let him have a red light; they don't permit them on posse members' cars.

Poor little Bailey Spratt, with no red light, not even a siren. Of course, with his automobile agency, he could start an ambulance service, and drive the ambulance himself on the chauffeur's day off.

Now Bailey Spratt said: 'Who's the dame? You're married, I met your wife one time. Who's the dame you're smooching around with on city time?'

Coming from that red, angry face, the juvenile expression was too much for me. 'Live happy, Mr. Spratt,' I said. 'Don't be mad all the time. It'll shorten your life.' It was flippant, but it left him silent long enough for me to get back in the car and back away; if I'd gone forward, I'd have ruined some paint for the city and for Mr. Spratt's car — a demonstrator, I suppose.

Miss Crowther was still asleep in the car as I got to her house. It was a C-3 model, and I noticed something; there were two names on the door. She lived with some other girl.

C-3s have two bedrooms. I couldn't tell which was hers, though they had different color schemes. If I'd known more about women, I would have been able to tell what colors a brunette would choose, I suppose, but then I didn't know much about women . . .

Finally, I just put her down on the couch in the living room, pulled a pink throw-blanket from the foot of one of the beds, and covered her over. On second thought, I took her shoes off. First aid procedure said I should loosen any tight clothing, like a girdle or brassiere. I didn't.

Now I was worried. I'd called her doctor when she looked tired and maybe in danger of having a breakdown; what she had now was much more serious. So I called Dr. Barnhart's number, and got his office nurse. Dr. Barnhart was still in the city. I asked: 'Who takes his calls? Dr. Levy?'

'Why, no. Dr. Crossen.'

'He's a pediatrician.'

The nurse said she knew that. She sounded a little annoyed with me. Then she said: 'Dr. Barnhart has started home from the hospital. He ought to be here in a few minutes. He's a very fast driver.'

Then she said: 'Oh, I mean, he never exceeds the speed limit, of course — '

'Okay, okay. I leave traffic to my betters.'

'You just stay there, lieutenant, and I'll send the doctor around the minute he shows up.'

I got a chair and pulled it over by the couch. Miss Crowther was rolling around a little, and moaning. When she flung her arm out, the hand groping, I took her hand and held it tight. She returned the pressure, and it seemed to calm her. She said, very clearly: 'Oh, Walt, you've come back to me,' and brought my hand up to her mouth and kissed it. Now I wanted to get out of there. This was something I had no right to hear. Walt Adams was my friend, Ellie Adams was my friend. If Walt was having an affair with his assistant, I wanted to hear it from him or not at all.

The half-conscious dame was getting restless; I suppose she could feel my attention slipping away from her. Her legs thrashed, and the throw rug fell away, disclosing long legs in beige nylons. I had been right; she had a girdle on, and according to the first aid manual this was not good for people in comas or semi-comas. But I was damned if I'd take it off her.

The way my luck was running, the Ladies Guild of the United Churches of Naranjo Vista would walk in and catch me right in the middle of the act. 'She's just a snot-nosed brat,' the lady assistant principal said. 'I knew you'd see through her, Walt dear. I'm so happy.'

I reached down and covered her attractive legs. The thing to do was to phone for our public nurse, Miss Hellman. Or look up the housemate and get her to come home.

The educator on the couch was dropping into obscenity. She was saying that she knew how to perform the sexual act better than any teenaged bitch, to paraphrase as nicely as my limited vocabulary will permit me.

The phone was there in the living room. If I could spare Miss Hellman, I ought to; we'd routed her out last night for the Pattersons.

I opened the front door, read the housemate's name again. Virginia McManus. The phone book had her listed only for this address, no business phone. There was a personal telephone directory, hand written; but she wasn't under V or M . . . I phoned the station, told the duty sergeant to get a business address for Virginia McManus, and gave him the number where I was, which I should have done the minute I got out of the car and off the short wave radio.

Miss Crowther was now detailing all the things she would like to or was willing to do for Walt. Miss Crowther certainly had an M.A. in order to be assistant principal of a high school. Maybe she had a Ph.D. But she was unable to think of any more filth than a guttersnipe.

The station called back. No business number for Virginia McManus. They had checked with the fire department, and in case of fire Miss Eleanor Crowther was to be notified at the high school.

Of course, many men were named Walter.

So I had a right and a duty to search the place. And, dammit, I should have done it before. Except that a Walt-Eleanor-Ellie triangle was none of my business. That is, not police business.

But I wanted to know. I wanted to prove to myself that the Walt of Miss Crowther's mutterings was not my friend, but a completely different Walter. Maybe Walter Ulbricht, or Walter Reuther.

Of course, it wasn't. The second bureau drawer I opened had a picture of Walt in it, in a silver frame, lying on its back among handkerchiefs and bobby pins and so on.

Which proved I was in the wrong room to find out about Miss (Mrs.?) Virginia McManus. It also proved some other things.

In the other room, the pink and silver one, a very quick search turned up an envelope addressed to Miss Virginia, at Industrial Statistics, Inc., in the city. My high-powered detective training carried me back to the phone book, and my highly-trained finger dialed the long distance necessary to get I.S., Inc., and Miss McManus was in.

A good enough girl for a policeman to call. She didn't squawk when I told her that there'd been a fire at the high school and her roommate had had a collapse and needed help, preferably feminine help. She said she'd be home within the hour.

For the ninetieth time, I regretted that Jack Davis's prejudices had kept us from replacing some policewomen who had gone sour on us. We had to get Miss Hellman on the rare occasions when we wanted to search a female. A nice blue-skirted cop would have been a lovely thing to check this mess to.

I had not given Miss Crowther the pills that Dr. Barnhart advised. She didn't seem to need sedation; she was as dopey as necessary already.

If anything, she needed something to stimulate her, but all that could wait till Barnhart got there. Me, I needed stimulation, too. I went into the kitchen. Nothing but powdered coffee — two dames, living alone, with no man to cook for — but it would do; I put on water.

Then I took a look at the patient. Legs and girdle were again visible, and as before, they did little for me. Last night I had liked this girl, but not now, which was silly.

No, not silly. Silly — Olga was bringing me up to her level — was an omnibus word. The word I wanted was prudish. Because this girl had fallen in love with a married man, because she was sexually ingenious in trying to hold him, I had no right to look down on her. I was a cop, not a reformer. People's sex lives were their own, so long as they didn't endanger the public peace.

My water was boiling. I took a cup of the powdered brew straight, scalding hot. It made little beads of sweat pop out on my forehead, but it made me feel better. I was washing the cup when the front doorbell rang.

Doctor — thank God — Barnhart. I told him who I was, let him in, and led him to the couch. I said: 'I'm checking it to you, doctor. I've called her house mate,

Miss McManus. She's on her way home.'

He nodded. 'Do I smell coffee, lieutenant?'

'Powdered. In the kitchen. I just had a cup.'

'Make me one, will you? One sugar, no cream.'

It wasn't an order. He was just used to having a nurse or an intern or an orderly or someone following him; when he wanted something he asked for it: 'Scalpel. Coffee. Handkerchief. Forceps.'

This was a time when Andy Bastian needed all the friends he could make. I went and boiled more water, and brought him his cup.

He was just putting a needle back in his black bag, pulling the covers over Miss Crowther's much-viewed legs. He said: 'You know when they go into one of these withdrawal-from-reality kicks, it's best to help them really get there. It's something your wife will never be able to do, it seems?'

Probably I said: 'Huh?'

'You're Olga Bastian's husband, aren't you? Sit down, Andy. You don't mind my calling you that? I'm quite a lot older than you are.'

'Probably not.' He had a little white at the temples, but all the hair was there, and what wrinkles he had looked like they'd come from laughing. 'I'm twelve years older than Olga.'

'And twelve years younger than I am. Also, you are nine feet tall, four feet across at the shoulders, have an I.Q. of 2043, are slightly handsomer than any movie star, and should be the head of the combined FBI, CIA and possibly the President's Cabinet. Olga talks about you often.'

So I sat down, and tried to pull my eyebrows down at the same time.

'Olga has had courses under me,' he explained. 'In fact, the year before she met you, she was my teaching assistant.'

'That makes me a hell of a cop. Barnhart isn't so common a name that I shouldn't have figured it out. Professor Barnhart, Doctor Barnhart. Sure. The same guy.'

He laughed. 'All right. I've wanted to

talk to you. Hal Levy said he would, has he?'

'I know Hal. We talk about a lot of things.'

The professor stared at me until I was a little ashamed of getting hard-nosed. But until I saw where this was going, I wanted to play it cosy.

'Well, this,' he said. 'We both think it's a shame that Olga doesn't try for her M.D. Hal says she doesn't because she doesn't want to be a perpetual schoolgirl, and a burden on you, financially.'

'The money doesn't mean a damned thing,' I said. 'I make plenty. Levy's offered her a partnership.'

'Oh, yes,' he said. 'Hal doesn't know the first thing about psychiatry. I suspect that in a few years, Olga would be the important partner ... But she should have own medical degree.' He gestured toward the couch. 'What would she do if one of her patients were in this condition? Phone for an intern? As a lay analyst, a clinical psychologist, she'd never have the right to use a needle, or even prescribe a pill.'

'When I phoned you, I thought you were Miss Crowther's family doctor,' I said. 'I didn't realize you were a screw-tightener.'

'There's a flattering term, flatfoot.'

We both grinned. I should have been thinking of Olga, but I wasn't. The knowledge that Miss Crowther was having mental trouble — not the right term, but it will do — *and* an affair with Walt Adams was very possibly police business. Crime prevention department.

High schools are focal points for crime. Maybe they didn't used to be, but they are now. Ours didn't seem to be in the best hands — a principal who had had an affair with his assistant and then with some other girl, and an assistant principal with a breakdown because she had been spurned for a younger woman. This did not make for the close attention school kids, high school kids particularly, need. I got ready to pump Dr. Barnhart. I wanted to find out just how unstable Miss Crowther was.

'I've wanted to meet you for a long time,' Dr. Barnhart was saying.

My mind came back to my own problems, away from those of the police department. 'If I lay a little — whatsit, a psychologic block — problem in your lap, doctor, do I get sent a bill?'

He let me make what I wanted to out of a smile.

'This, then. I'm very anxious for Olga to go for her medical degree. It would take about four years, wouldn't it?'

'Including her internship, yes. But I don't see the problem. You and I are in complete agreement.'

'Without trying to use any of the terms Olga's taught me, my motives are pretty badly mixed. In fact, when I take a good look at them, I come up thinking I'm a stinker . . . Like this, doc. So long as Olga's a student and I'm a big shot assistant police chief, I'm high mucka-muck around her house. When she's a practicing doctor, M.D. or Ph.D., I'm just her lowbrow cop husband. So I'd like her to keep studying for the next twenty or thirty years. In other words, I'm a stinker.'

His head went back to laugh, exposing his strong throat. On the couch, Miss

Crowther stirred, and the doctor choked his laugh off, went to take her hand, feel her pulse. Then he poked one of her eyelids up, and shook his head. 'She's fighting the sedative,' he said. 'That's one of the things a double-doctor like Olga could find out about. A straight M.D. like Hal Levy, now, has to go on the assumption that dosage is dosage, no matter what the mental condition of the patient is. That simply isn't so.'

'You haven't answered my question.'

'Well, I'll answer one of them; you don't get a bill . . . The other one is more difficult. Let me start out by saying I'm flattered you brought it to me . . . '

'But — '

He raised his hand. 'Unlike Olga, I am neither a clinical psychologist nor a psychoanalyst. I'm a psychiatrist, which really means just a medical man who has decided to specialize in mental and nervous disorders. I should have had many more courses in philosophy, for instance, before being confronted with a problem like yours. Let me talk around it for a while.'

'Go ahead,' I said. But I was thinking, here I am on duty, and wasting time talking about myself and my wife. Bailey Spratt ought to know about this; he could really make something of it.

'Our Russian friends say that the end justifies the means,' Dr. Barnhart said. 'So if Olga goes to medical school, the reason doesn't matter. But we're not in Russia. If we were, I imagine you wouldn't have the problem, anyway. A police officer would be so much higher than anyone else, he wouldn't have to worry.'

'When you say you're going to talk around a subject, you mean way around, don't you, doc?'

'Please don't call me doc. Al, if you must be intimate.'

He wasn't being funny. I got red in the face; I'm not used to being put in my place that way. But it was like his order to make him a cup of coffee; it was said and forgotten as soon as he'd said it. By him, at least. I remembered it.

'We in the United States, are under a very peculiar system,' the doctor went on.

'A cop is as good as an atomic physicist, the milkman can catch as many fish as the banker. Only, of course, it's not so. The physicist calls up the police chief, or the mayor, and the cop is in trouble; the banker owns the trout stream, and the milkman is arrested for trespassing.'

'Doctor, doctor, come down to earth.'

He nodded. 'Money and status are the carrots that make the American run,' he said. 'First, money. I don't imagine the top ranking police officer in the United States, the head of the FBI or the New York Police Department, makes more than twenty-five thousand dollars a year. As the sort of practitioner I expect Olga to become, she could readily make three times that much. I don't think she will, because she is Olga, and before she reaches that goal, she is going to start devoting most of her time to clinical and research work, which doesn't pay at all. But she'll undoubtedly be able to make more than you.'

He was levelling with me at last. I owed him a slow answer; I turned one over in my mind, until I was satisfied with it, and then spoke it. 'Not too important. I'll be paying my own way. And I can always remind myself that my earnings paid her way through college.'

'Good answer,' he said, putting me back in the orphan school again. 'Very good answer. Now, status. Unless you've lost confidence in yourself, you ought to be more important four years from now than you are now. And you're pretty important, now. Even an ex-ambulance rider like me is slightly awed by a police lieutenant. Now, we face a simple question, and then we're done: do you think you'll be a bigger man four years from now, or don't you? Because if you do, your motives are pure; if you don't, you're simply postponing a decision, which means eventual trouble and probably the breakup of your marriage.'

'If I didn't think I was getting some place, I'd go back in the Army and buck for colonel,' I said.

And then I realized that he had solved my problem for me, by making me do it myself, and all at once I realized what Olga's profession was all about. I felt fine, and I said: 'I know now why you're a professor.'

'Thanks,' he said, 'and now that the interview is over, you can call me doc, if you want to. I was establishing prestige over you, in the cant of my trade.'

I stood up, put out my hand. 'What does Olga call you?'

He laughed, more gently than before, and with a quick look at Miss Crowther. 'When she was my assistant she called me, 'prof.' when she liked me and 'Dockie' when she was mad.'

'Then, thanks, prof.'

He took my hand and then he held it. He looked at the ceiling. 'The subject of status,' he said. 'It's one I'd like to talk about at length with you.'

'We'll do that, prof. But just at the moment, I'm on duty. I've wasted too much time on myself now.'

But he hung onto my hand. 'What makes a man become a teacher?' he asked the ceiling. 'For the same investment in time and money, he could have gotten a law degree or a medical one, both paying much better than teaching does.'

'Maybe he lives in a town where there's a teacher's college and not a law school.'

Dr. Barnhart shook his head. 'That's a sort of superficial answer. But assuming something like that, how does it feel to be a high school principal, or a school superintendent, and to be at the beck and call — to coin a phrase — of every rich ass in town when you're educated and think you're successful?'

'Sounds like you're acquainted with Bailey Spratt, prof.'

He shook his head. 'The car dealer? I just know his name on the window of his garage or agency or whatever it is.'

I am not fast. I was never trained to be fast, except with a gun or my fist, or a nightstick. I was trained to take it easy, to absorb one fact at a time, to be sure of everything I said before I said it, and not to judge by appearances or jump to conclusions. That is what makes a good policeman, not being brilliant or running around faster than anyone else. But I was beginning to get something, fast or not, smart or not. 'Doctor, do you know Walt Adams?'

He nodded.

I said: 'Is there something you want to tell me?'

Dr. Barnhart shook his head. He said: 'What a doctor learns from a patient is as sacred as what a priest learns from a confessing communicant. I imagine there are things picked up in police work that can never be disclosed to anyone. This conversation, lieutenant, cannot continue without getting into unethical country.'

'Well, thanks for the advice.'

'Advice always pleasures the giver more than the receiver. You say Miss Crowther's roommate will be home soon?'

Nodding, I asked: 'How long has she been a patient of yours?'

He shrugged, and turned away, and went to sit next to her. Me, I went out and got in my car and sat there and was almost sick to my stomach. Something had finally penetrated my thick brain.

Walt Adams, my friend, was now prime suspect in the rape of Nora Patterson.

13

My drive to Walt's house was slow. I did not relish what I was about to do, what I had to do: take the bandage off Walt's face, and, if he was scratched up, take him into custody.

The long dreary procedure stretched ahead of me. The interview with the district attorney. The examination of Walt by Sergeant Ernen, possibly by official doctors. The Press interviews . . .

And — oh, God — the arrest of Dr. Hal Levy, Harold Levy, M.D. Because if Walt's face was scratched, Hal had withheld police information. He had been told we were looking for a man in Naranjo Vista whose face was scratched; he had been told it by me, officially.

The law is very specific. What a patient tells a doctor is sacred, all right, unless the patient tells it to a doctor employed by the police or the district attorney, and knows at the time whom the doctor is working for.

But what a doctor sees, that is different. Failure to report a gunshot wound is withholding information from the police, and under some situations, has been construed as harboring a fugitive.

Failure to report a scratched face when informed that the police are looking for a man with a scratched face would be withholding information, harboring and aiding a criminal, and possibly becoming an accessory after the fact. Hal Levy would be indicted, and he probably would lose his medical license or his membership in the county Medical Association or both.

The accessory charge was a felony rap.

So it was no wonder I drove slowly. I had been worried about Olga and Hal Levy; I was still not sure that there wasn't something there. Had Dr. Barnhart been trying to tell me not to let Olga go into partnership with Hal, or I'd lose her? The prof. was not a straight talker; I wasn't sure.

But what I had to do, I'd do. I was not about to let a rapist go because he was a

214

friend of mine, or because I didn't want my wife getting angry with me for making trouble for her friend.

There was the Adams house, and the Adams driveway. I parked the car and went in to do my duty, and let the friends fall where they fall. I hadn't chosen to be an MP, but I had surer than hell made my own choice about going on with a police career, and here we paid for it.

I rang the Adams's bell.

Ellie came to the door. Her face lit up with a real smile when she saw me. She put both hands on my forearm, and gave me a little squeeze. 'Andy, how nice to see you. Have you come to see Walt? He's asleep, thank goodness.'

'Wake him up,' I said.

Her smile faded. 'Why, Andy, are you out of your mind? You know how Walt is when he's just got a cold and — '

'May I see him, Mrs. Adams? I can get a warrant if I have to.'

Her face was awful — pale and staring and wan. I pushed past her and into the master bedroom, Plan C-2, Bartlett Construction Company.

The bed was empty. It was not only empty, it was made up, unruffled.

Ellie had hold of my arm again, but not now in friendship or in flirtation. She was babbling nonsense.

I shook her off and looked in the guest room, just to be sure, but he wasn't there. I said: 'When did he scram?'

She shrieked: 'You Cossack,' at me. I have been called that before.

Her shoulders were knobs under my hands as I grabbed her and shook her. 'Make sense, Ellie. The longer he runs, the worse the case against him gets.'

She struck at my face. She didn't claw, I noticed as I weaved my head to avoid her; she made fists and tried strike like a man. It wasn't very effective.

Finally I shoved her away from me, and crossed to the phone. She collapsed into a big chair — Walt's favorite — and began to cry, a thin, horrible, wailing noise.

The number of the police station had gone out of my head. I think I was more shocked by that than by anything else that had happened. I had to look in the phone book, and there it was, on the first page under Emergency Listings and I dialled it.

Sergeant McRaine was on duty. He said: 'Naranjo Vista Police,' loud and clear, and his sensible, everyday voice brought me back to earth. 'This is Lieutenant Bastian,' I said.

At once he said: 'Captain Davis has been looking for you,' and his switches clicked and his lines buzzed, and Jack Davis said: 'Andy, get in here at once.'

'Listen, Jack — '

'I said at once, damn it,' and the phone clicked

The instrument was heavy in my hands. I hung it back in its cradle and turned back. 'Listen, Ellie, you've got to help me. It'll be much easier on Walt if I can find him and say he surrendered to me than if I have to put out an All Points Bulletin. You can see that.'

She wailed: 'I don't know. He just — he just said that everything was ruined and I was never to see him again, and he ran out.'

'When was this?'

'About nine-thirty this morning.'

So now I knew who had burned the desk in Walt's office; Walt himself. Who'd notice something so common as the principal going into the principal's office? There wouldn't be time to sort out whatever evidence about Eleanor Crowther and Nora Patterson was in the desk — so burn the whole thing.

'Where do you think he'd run to?' But she was crying again.

Then, through her wet fingers, she blurted: 'He took his gun. His service automatic.'

I stared at her. I patted her back. There wasn't anything to say, so I left without saying it.

My police chief had ordered me into the station fast; I'd better go. As I trotted for my car, I looked at my watch. Olga would be home from college in an hour; I'd send her over to be with Ellie. It was no job for a nurse, and Hal Levy was the Adams's doctor. Dr. Levy would not be available. Someone else would have to take his calls.

I didn't have to use the siren or the red light to get to the station; Naranjo Vista was in a quiet, traffic-free mood. I coasted into the basement garage and used the stairs to get up to the street level.

The patrolman in Jack Davis's office jerked a thumb at the inner door, and I went on through.

Jack Davis was not alone. There was a small, very dapper old gent in one of his visitors' chairs, a burly, athletic looking guy of about thirty-five in the other.

Jack's greeting wasn't like him: 'Where the hell have you been, lieutenant?'

I pulled myself up, threw him a ball, though I was in plainclothes. 'Out on duty, sir. The Patterson case. I want to see you alone, at once, sir.'

'Let that all go,' Jack Davis said. 'This is Mr. Wright. This is his lawyer, Mr. Leonard. Mr. Wright is the father of the prisoner who called himself John Davis.'

Mr. Wright said: 'I don't understand that. Not at all. As though he was ashamed of his name.'

'It's my name,' Jack said. 'He probably thought it was funny, giving the police chief's name for the blotter. They — '

Whoever 'they' were or what 'they' did,

he decided not to talk about. He looked red-faced and angry. He glared at me. 'Get yourself a chair, lieutenant.'

He'd never called me that before. 'I'll stand.'

Mr. Wright said: 'He had a great sense of humor, Junie did . . . We called him Junie, for Junior, lieutenant. He was always laughing.'

They always are, on Skid Row. Light, empty, meaningless giggles are the theme song of the lush, the bum and the moocher. It had been many years since I had thought that laughter meant they were happy.

'How could you do it?' Mr. Wright asked, suddenly. 'You had my boy in charge. How could you let him get shot?'

I said: 'Captain, could I see you outside a minute?'

Jack Davis said: 'We have visitors, Bastian. 'I — ' I guess he could read the rising anger in my face. 'Excuse me, gentlemen.'

When we got outside, he blared out at me. 'Where the hell have you been? I've had the worst half hour of my life with that old foop. You picked a fine time to go corking off someplace.'

'I'm not a rookie patrolman, Jack. I'm not a raw recruit out of high school. Listen. Walt Adams has taken it on the lam, and I think he raped the Patterson girl.' I gave it to him hard and straight. I made an official report out of it, the way we had been trained to do. The only thing I left out was Dr. Barnhart's part; it didn't seem to apply, and the doctor had been slightly unethical in tipping me off. He'd been disclosing information he'd gotten while treating Miss Crowther. I let Jack think that Miss Crowther had used Nora Patterson's name, but she hadn't, she'd only referred to a young bitch, or words to that effect.

My neck was out again.

Jack Davis nodded, and leaned against the corridor wall. The red was ebbing out of his face. He fished in his pockets — he was wearing a sun tan uniform — and got out cigarettes and matches. He held my light for me. Then he cleared his throat, and said: 'You're the hell of a police officer, aren't you, Andy? You can smell your way through a case, and come up with the right answer when all the rest of us are looking around for our shoes to put on.'

'No. You told me to take Miss Crowther home. I did. When I got there, she didn't seem in shape to leave alone. So I stayed, and she talked.'

He didn't seem to hear me. 'You put out an APB yet?'

'No. Half an hour doesn't matter. Walt Adams isn't going to go assaulting anyone else. And if he was going to kill himself, he would have done it before I ever heard of it.

Jack Davis nodded. 'Yeah, I can see that.' He walked down the corridor, and opened Drew Lasley's door without knocking. 'Drew, there's a beef in my office. The father of the punk that Norman Patterson shot. Go talk to him. He's probably going to sue us, and Andy here in particular, but try and get him to do it for a nice, small amount.'

'Jack,' I said, as Drew went by us to take the duty, 'I'm glad you think this is funny.'

'We got to decide what to do about Walt,' Jack Davis said. 'C'mon in your office.'

So we went there. I was beginning to get the pitch. It was all my grief. Jack Davis was the chief, he was captain of our jolly little force, but if Walt Adams got away, it was because I hadn't put him on the air as soon as I suspected him. If, on the other hand, he was picked up and proved innocent, it was all my fault, too.

Jack rambled along, saying nothing, but issuing a number of words. I reached for my phone. 'Get me Dr. Levy.'

Jack Davis was saying: 'Mr. Bartlett said he'd back you all the way. Maybe a private detective agency instead — '

'Captain, either check this to me, or don't.'

I'd never spoken to him that way. He got red in the face again, and then he said: 'I'm your superior officer.'

'Don't I — ' I broke off. We sounded childish.

Dr. Levy's phone had been ringing. Now the ringing stopped, and his voice said name and title. I said my own name, without title, but I added: 'This is police business. Walt Adams has skipped.'

Dr. Harold Levy waited a second and then said: 'Oh.'

'There's a strong chance you're in trouble, doctor. Was his face scratched?'

A longer silence and then: 'Yes. It could have been fingernails. He could also have run into a tree in the dark. There are some locust saplings on the school grounds . . . '

'Cut it, doc. Why didn't you report this?'

No waiting at all this time. Hal said: 'Because Walt Adams could never commit rape in a million years, no matter how much the provocation. And I didn't want him framed.'

'This department doesn't frame people.'

'No,' he said, 'but it jumps to conclusions, just like all cops, everywhere and every place. And having made its conclusions, it backs them up. If cops were professional men with some training, some education, I might have told you. But you — they — are simply guys with broad shoulders and long legs and blackjacks and guns. I don't believe in turning my friends over to them.'

And there it was. This was what the world thought of us, this was what Olga's friends really thought of Olga's husband. When the chips were down, a cop was all alone in a world that didn't like him.

'Got any idea where Walt is, doctor?'

'No.'

'Okay, pal. I'll find him. And when I do I'll probably get a confession out of him. And if that confession includes a statement that he told you where he was going, I'll take a keen, professional pleasure in chopping that M.D. off the end of your name so quick you'll think a surgeon with twenty years education did it. Okay?'

He slammed the phone down on the other end of the wire.

Jack Davis said: 'Hey, Andy, Dr. Levy's a big man in Naranjo Vista.'

'Don't I know it, captain? Don't I just know it?'

14

Now it was necessary to go back to Jack Davis's office and soothe Mr. Wright. It was our fault that his son was a wino and a peeping Tom and generally no good.

Everything in me wanted to take off in all directions at once and chase Walt Adams. But I couldn't do it; my loyalty to Jack demanded that I get Mr. Wright off his neck first.

Sure. I should have sent out a bulletin on Walt. But I thought, if one of those gun-hipped cops up in the city walked up on him, Walt was likely to kill himself, I didn't know what poisons would be in a high school chemistry lab, but if there were any, he would have helped himself.

And, with Walt dead, this case would fall apart again, as it had fallen apart when Sergeant Ernen ruled out little Junior Wright, the wino, as the man Nora Patterson had scratched.

One more mistake, and I was through.

This was the third strike.

So I put on my best face, and went back to Jack's office. Mr. Wright was still sitting; but his lawyer, Mr. Leonard, had gone around behind the captain's desk, and was staring out the window. His fingernails were drumming on the sill. Drew Lasley went out, fast.

Mr. Wright said: 'Really, this is unpardonable. We've been waiting and waiting, and my boy is lying in a hospital at death's door.'

Jack Davis said: 'I'm sorry, Mr. Wright. Something came up. You know how it is when you're running a police department.'

Reasonably enough, Mr. Wright said he didn't know. 'And I don't think you are running this one very well, letting my boy get shot.'

Jack Davis let that one go over his shoulder, and said: 'Well, as I told you, this is Lieutenant Bastian's case. I'm sure that he'll see you're taken care of.' Whatever that meant. 'Use the office as long as you want, Andy,' and he scrammed.

I sat down at Jack's desk. I made a speech: 'Mr. Wright, you are not a taxpayer here in Naranjo Vista. You have, so far as I know, no political influence. Your lawyer here, Mr. Leonard, has, perhaps, told you that under such circumstances, you can expect little cooperation from this force.' My God, listen to me. I should have been a preacher. Actually, I guess, I had been listening when the black coats lectured us kids in the orphanage. 'He couldn't be more wrong,' I went on. 'I want you to treat me exactly as though I worked for you. Tell me what you want, and if I can't do it, I'll tell you why.' I sat back and started to make a steeple out of my fingers, and then thought better of it.

Little Mr. Wright said: 'Well, now, that is more like it. I want to see my boy. At the hospital, they wouldn't let me see Junie.'

'No harm in that, but the hospital was right. Without permission from this department, or the district attorney, no one but his lawyer can see a prisoner. How was he, Mr. Leonard?'

The lawyer had said very little so far; which is not the way of lawyers. Since this guy might very possibly be suing me for letting little Junior Wright get shot. I was anxious to know him.

Now, to my amazement, his face was getting red. 'I didn't see him,' he said.

The amazement on my face was not put on. 'The hospital must be crazy,' I said. 'There's no way of keeping a lawyer from his client. Didn't you tell them that?'

'Mr. Wright, Jr., is not my client,' Leonard said.

'He won't have anything to do with us,' old Mr. Wright said. 'He thinks I ruined his life. He's a very bad boy, lieutenant.' And Mr. Wright began to cry.

Mr. Leonard mopped his face with a very large, very white handkerchief. I found Jack's box of tissues in his drawer, and gave it to Mr. Wright to cry into.

Then I reached for the phone. 'Get me the County Hospital, prison ward. I want to talk to whoever has charge of our prisoner, the one we booked as John Davis. His real name is

Something-or-other Wright, Junior.'

Mr. Wright said: 'Fitzroy. Our first name is Fitzroy.'

'Fitzroy Wright, Junior, Del,' I said to De Laune on the phone. I hung up.

'As you say, Mr. Wright, Junior is a bad boy. I caught him last night watching my wife take a bath, through the window. Since we'd just had a sex assault here — '

What I was going to explain was why Norman Patterson had shot Junior; but I never had a chance.

'Oh, Junie would never do that,' Mr. Wright cried. 'He's very popular with the girls. He can get all the girls he wants! Why, you can't believe how many of them there used to be, calling him up, chasing him all over the place. It's what I told those policemen — '

Mr. Leonard came to life. He cried: 'Stop it, Mr. Wright. This is a policeman you're talking to!'

Then they both shut up. I said: 'You'd better keep talking.'

Mr. Leonard gave me a lawyer's look — trained to give nothing away, but to remain genial and frank-looking at the same time. 'You have Mr. Wright, Jr.'s fingerprints, lieutenant. You know he has no record.'

'The hell he doesn't, counsellor. Los Angeles makes him six times, five drunk and disorderlys, one habitual drunkard. Long Beach makes him twice, drunk in a public place, and indecent exposure. The last can be made into a sex charge if we want to. There's another exposure charge out of Santa Monica.'

Mr. Leonard said: 'I know those police charges. Making water in an alley.'

I grinned: 'You're not Junior Wright's lawyer, why worry? In court, they could be made to stand up as a habitual sex deviate, together with the peeping Tom charge.'

Mr. Leonard said: 'Nonsense,' but his client started to cry again.

'You'd better talk to me,' I said. 'What you tell me I can use while I'm still in a good mood. What I have to dig out I might get when I'm hot and tired.'

'Treat me just as if I worked for you,'' Mr. Leonard said. 'Soft talk, police soft talk.'

Then the phone rang. I picked it up, and Mac said he had Dr. Eastman up at County. I said: 'Doctor, I've got the prisoner's father here. So far as our department goes, we have no objection to him seeing his son.'

'Oke, lieutenant,' Dr. Eastman said. He had an Eastern voice, New York or Philadelphia, and a lower class one. He sounded tough and cheerful. 'Want I should put a bug under the bed?'

'What?'

'I'm a hi-fi fan,' Dr. Eastman said. 'Not that being an intern gives me much time. I got microphones and things. I'd be glad to bug the bed for you.'

'No, thanks,' I said. But it was a temptation.

'I doubt if Junior will see the old man,' Dr. Eastman said. 'He wouldn't see the lawyer this morning. Called him the worst crook in Stockton. Sent his temperature up a notch.'

'How is the prisoner?'

'Not good,' the intern said. 'Dehydrated, devitaminized, and then shocked from loss of blood. Now, your other case, that prisoner Norman Patterson, whoever shot him would make a surgeon. I couldn't go through a thigh with less damage if I had a scalpel or an electric knife.'

'Thanks, pal. That was my work.'

'You're good,' the doc said. Then, off the phone he said: 'What?' and when he got back to me, said: 'County detective says Patterson's daughter came to, but she won't talk. Says she saw nothing.'

We exchanged so-longs, and I hung up. 'You heard that,' I said. 'You get to see your son whether you cooperate with me or not. If he wants to see you, which I gather he doesn't.'

'You could order him to,' Mr. Wright said. 'You're a police officer.'

'I could order you to talk, but you wouldn't. If your lawyer here told you I could order a prisoner to talk to his family, get a new lawyer.' And I gave Mr. Leonard my brightest smile.

'You knew I didn't say that,' he said.

'No. You know the law. Mr. Leonard, what was Junior — no, *when* was Junior picked up on a possible rape charge?'

He said: 'You have his record.'

'And it doesn't show there. But there are times when a man's arrest doesn't show. When he's dismissed and his family has influence.'

Mr. Leonard said: 'Let's get back to the hospital, Mr. Wright.'

They left without shaking hands.

Now, I could start looking for Walt Adams. But instead I leaned back in Jack's chair, and thought. Junior Wright's face was not scratched; his hair was not the same color as that found in Nora Patterson's fingers. He was not the man she'd fought with.

But he was the man who was shot in my custody. There still might be a case against me. And the worse Junior's record was, the cleaner I looked for bringing him into custody . . .

Jack Davis came in. 'Call me a coward,' he said. 'I hung out in the radio room till I saw they were gone . . . What's the matter, Andy?'

'Our wino friend was once picked up on a sexual assault charge. Somebody,

234

probably mouthpiece Leonard, got the thing off the blotter.'

Jack shrugged. 'We know he isn't the guy who attacked Nora,' he said. 'Walt Adams is.'

'Last night, in the garage at my place, we were sure the other way around.'

Then I remembered that I was in Captain Davis's chair. I got up and moved to the seat Mr. Wright had used.

Jack Davis made the swivel chair creak as he flung himself into it. 'What the hell are you trying to say, Andy? That the lab up at County goofed?'

'Did you meet that Sergeant Ernen? He doesn't goof.'

Jack's face began to glow red. 'You can't have it both ways. Me, I don't put a hell of a lot of faith in lab work; and on the other hand, you and this Ernen convinced me the little wino couldn't have done it. What do you want?'

'A clean case that will stand up in court. I want money to go up to Stockton and get the whole story on Junior Wright.'

Jack Davis slammed his flat hand down on his desk. 'This is a small department.'

'Mr. Bartlett wired that he'd stand behind us,'

'Behind you,' Jack Davis said. He was jealous; he was the chief, he didn't like the idea that I was getting too prominent. And maybe he kept remembering I'd been his superior in the Army, was still a grade over him in the Reserve. He stood up now, and pounded a clenched fist into the palm of the other hand. 'Mr. Bartlett is not going to be paying our way forever,' he said, 'The people who own houses here will be the taxpayers. It's up to us to cooperate with them.'

I looked at him. He had been my friend a long, long time. 'You joined the gun club, Jack?'

He returned my stare. 'I am chief of this force.'

And there we had it. Bailey Spratt had gotten to him. I didn't know how; maybe by offering him extra pay as an arms instructor to the gun club. Maybe by flaunting his political influence. Being an Inspector of Deputies was bigger than being chief of Naranjo Vista . . .

But my last friend was gone.

'Okay, Jack,' I said. 'Want to use my resignation?'

The red had been ebbing; now it flooded back into his full cheeks. 'Don't be a damned fool, Andy. What'll you do? Go back into the Army and be sent overseas while Olga takes a room in a college dormitory?'

'I've been handed a case. I want to run it out my own way. Okay, you don't want to spend money; but I'll pay my own way to Stockton, when I finish up a thing or two here. We'll take up the resignation when I finish this case.

'Put out an APB on Walt Adams, and you can close it tonight. And forget the resignation.'

'Walt Adams has a gun,' I said. 'If he's crowded, he'll kill himself.'

Jack Davis swung around his chair until he was looking out the window at peaceful, sunny Naranjo Vista. Over his shoulder, he finally said: 'Well?'

'I don't close cases that way.'

Jack Davis shook his head. 'This damned suburb has got you soft. You're a cop, not a Boy Scout. With Walt Adams dead and the case closed, we can all go back to getting along with each other. He was your friend, sure, but look what he did.'

'If he did it.'

'His own wife, his own doctor admitted he had scratches on his face. And he lammed. He's not your pal the gentle school teacher anymore; he's a felon, a rapist.'

'When a jury says he is.' But I sounded sour, even to myself. I'd gotten mad, and because of that I was talking like a — I don't know what. Police experience told me you couldn't always go by the book, but here I was, talking like a book cop . . . That was it. I had always had the greatest contempt for book cops. The way to work is to do what you have to do, and then fix the record to show you did it the regulation way. I said: 'If you want to put out an APB on Walt, do so. But do it yourself, or order me to do it in writing. If you want the investigation of Junior Wright stopped, put that in writing, too.'

Jack Davis said: 'Did you ever try cracking walnuts with that nose of yours?'

and before he'd finished, his phone had rung. He picked it up.

The voice on the other end was hearty; I could hear it clearly. It said: 'Hi, chief, this is your friend Bailey Spratt . . . '

I walked out of Jack Davis's office, and left the pieces of an old, old friendship on the floor.

My car was out back; I told the duty sergeant I was going home, and went. Olga was there. Usually I managed to pick her up at the bus stop when she got home from school, but this wasn't usually.

She wasn't alone. Her pal Hal Levy was in my living room, and they were drinking coffee together. I stood in the middle of the living room floor and said: 'Get out of here.'

Hal Levy blinked. Olga said: 'Take your hat off, Andy.'

I took my hat off and threw it on the couch. Then I took off my coat and threw it after the hat. I said: 'Doctor, get out, or I'll throw you out.' My wife was regarding me with a strange, strange look.

Hal Levy stood up. He said. 'Andy, you

239

need some rest. What have I done? I might even have been acting within my ethics.'

'You covered for Walt Adams. That's withholding evidence from the police. Okay. But Walt Adams has scrammed, taking a gun with him, and some cop is liable to be shot picking Walt off. Or Walt is just as liable to turn the gun on himself.'

'More liable,' Olga said. 'Walt wouldn't hurt anyone.'

'Don't give me any of your psychology,' I said, 'Walt Adams raped the Patterson girl!'

'Stop yelling at me,' Olga said.

Now I was not only a Boy Scout, but the den mother was bawling me out; I'd been demoted to Cub. I said: 'Okay, okay.'

Hal Levy opened his mouth, looked at me, and shut it again.

Olga said: 'If Walt lost his temper, he might hit somebody. But rape — it's out of the question.'

'What do you know?'

'I'm a psychologist,' Olga said. 'Also,

I'm a girl. I know.'

'Oh, my good Lord.' I went across the room and picked up my hat and jacket, carried them out. Over my shoulder I said: 'Hang around, doc. You and the little woman can discuss my psychopathic personality.'

That wasn't a bad crack; it made me feel a little better. A shower shoved me along the road. I noticed that Olga had pulled the shade in the bathroom all the way down and fastened it.

When I came out, Olga had on a pair of black slacks and a cherry-red sweater and had pulled her hair back in a long pony tail. She said: 'There's coffee hot. Take some.' Dr. Hal Levy had dematerialized.

'What in the world are you doing in those slacks? I didn't even know you owned them.'

'Oh, I got them once when I wanted to look like Jane College. Instead, I decided they made me look forty instead of thirty.'

'Twenty-seven,' I said, automatically.

She grinned. 'You're feeling better. Shall we go?'

'Huh?'

'Skid Row,' Olga said. 'I don't look like I'm dressed for the opera, do I?'

I shook my head. 'How in the world — '

'Where else would Walt be?'

'Tijuana. Oregon. Down at San Pedro, looking for a boat to China.'

Olga said: 'Do you really believe that, Andy? Walt isn't running away; he's the type that would be anxious to be punished. But first he has to debase himself. Walt's got a limited imagination and a limited body of information. He wouldn't know any place lower than Skid Row in Los Angeles.'

'I got a pretty extensive body of information, and I wouldn't know any place much lower myself.' I realized I was still popping my eyes at her. 'You figured this all out with psychology?'

'Sure,' Olga said. 'Well, the clothes you got out helped me.' I had pulled on my gardening slacks and an old Army windbreaker. 'How did you figure it out?'

'Some things I don't figure. I just go by past experience.'

'One way or the other,' Olga said, 'we

manage to have togetherness. How much of a job is it to search Skid Row?'

'Leadpipe cinch. About a mile long, maybe a hundred bars. And the guys drift, they don't stay in one place. We drift, too; we'll see every bum who hasn't passed out, in the course of a couple of hours. They just drift, I don't know why.'

'I'll explain it to you sometime,' my psychologist wife said. 'And don't say I'm not going. You're Walt's friend, but you're a policeman. If he sees you, he might do something foolish. If I put the collar on him, he'll go along like a little angel.'

'The angelic rapist,' I said.

'Walt is not a rapist,' Olga said firmly, and I followed her to the front door.

15

Skid Row is no longer on Main Street in L.A.; it has moved a couple of blocks east. We left the car in a parking lot, and hit the skids.

The road to hell is not glamorous. It has neon lights in all colors — rich reds and deep greens and electric blues and hard, sunny yellows — and it has noise — the noise of juke boxes, of three-men cowboy bands, of squabbles in the bars that don't pay for music, but depend on their neighbors.

It had smells, certainly. Smells of unwashed men, of Woolworth-perfumed women, of greasy hamburger frying in its own ample fat, and of potatoes frying in never changed cottonseed oil, and over all the smell of cheap, sugary wine and of vomited, half-digested beer.

It has no sights, unless people are sights; it's just the one sight over and over again, the slack face, the giggling mouth, the un-laughing eyes, the faint gleam of cold-sweat on pallid skin. There are no males and no females among the bums; just things that used to have sex.

We tramped from bar to bar, drinking bar whiskey, water on the side, a tight-pants Jill and her out-at-the knees Jack.

You don't get drunk on one shot of bar whiskey on Skid Row. The stuff's eighty proof, all right, or maybe eighty-six, but the sham glass has a thick bottom, and the line stops at half an ounce.

But you get a headache, or at last I do, but then, liquor has seldom done a thing for me.

Olga was different. A martini girl, she and her friends need a few to get going on their endless, happy, learned discussions. Eight of these drinks were just about the equal of two home-mixed martinis, I figured; and after a block or two, Olga was animated and beginning to enjoy herself.

'Look at that one,' she said. We were just crossing a street, about to embark on our third dreary block. A wind had come up, and papers, dust and frying smells whipped around us.

'That one,' was a very young man. He ambled along with his mouth open, a little shine of saliva at the edge of his lips. His filthy hula shirt was out around his hips, his Cotton cord slacks were shiny with grease. His hard eyes were on the ground; they shone under a mat of blond hair.

Behind him a pace or so ambled another lad, almost as spectacular, but a little cleaner.

'Shut your mouth, Jack,' I said. 'You're over-acting.'

The hard eyes glinted at me a moment, and then he had ambled past. But the mouth shut. 'I'll show you their car,' I said to Olga.

'What's this all about?'

'Undercover cops,' I said. 'Rookies assigned to the Narcotics Squad, trying to make a buy. Any sober guy would spot them, but some of the small-time pushers are hopheads or winos themselves.'

'But they'd never arrest anyone worth catching.'

'I know. But they keep the small-fry on the go, and besides, it's a good way of shaking out rookies who aren't really going to like police work once they're trained. Don't give it more than a passing glance, but see the hand-pencilled number on that license plate? Police car. Here. Watch how these cops don't look at it.'

Los Angeles, like most southwestern cities, does not go in for foot patrol, a modernization I don't agree with. But Skid Row can't be handled from a car; so down the street came two more rookies, uniformed ones, walking tall and proud in their summer blues, guns at their belts, night sticks in their hands, badges freshly polished.

They scanned the license plate of every car they passed, looking for stolen vehicles; that is, they did till they came to the pencilled police car. Then they snapped their heads away and looked at the bar-fronts for a car's length before they resumed their scrutiny.

'Rookies,' I said. I was laughing. 'They'll snap right-dress again when they pass the Narcotics Squad kids.'

'Yours is such a glamorous profession,' Olga said.

'Well, at least, I've never had to carry bedpans in the state insane asylum to study it. I'll buy you a drink in here.'

'If they'd used the bedpans, it wouldn't have been so bad,' Olga said. 'A big drink, daddy?'

This bar was called the T-Star, for some reason; all the worse bars had names, unlike the worst ones. It stood between a row of three hock shops and a dollar-shirt store. We turned in, unconsciously bracing ourselves with deep chests-full of the stale street air.

'Two whiskies, water back,' I told the bartender.

He was fat looking, but only at first glance; then you saw that the bulge under the cowboy shirt was hard as a drum, that the pudgy-looking arms were tightly muscled. He gave us the same sort of look we'd gotten on the other two blocks; whiskey is not often ordered on Skid Row. The scrawny tall guy on my right was drinking Green Death, which is a cheap, strong ale; the two fat bimbos past Olga were both indulging in a little cream sherry, not from Spain. By the time they get to the Row, their stomachs are usually too riddled to swallow hard liquor; the sugar in the wine, the grain in the beer is necessary.

The barman was looking at Olga. Without make-up, with her beatnik hairdo, she looked gaunt enough to him, I guess. He said: 'Two shnapps, water onna side.'

I turned my back on him, put my elbows on the bar, looked the room over. A bum was asleep on a splintery table, his head on his arm, his legs sprawled under the table as though they were broken. For a moment he looked a little like Walt Adams, and I half pushed away from the bar; then I saw it wasn't.

'Pay the man, daddy,' Olga said.

Turning, I put four bits on the bar in small change. It was not sipping whiskey; we gulped, and were glad of the chasers. I was beginning to get indigestion.

'Let's roll, babe,' I said.

'I'm not oiled yet, daddy,' she said.

'You promised to get me good and oiled.'

'That's a good girl,' the bartender said. 'You sell him, now.'

But something in her voice had caught me. I looked at her, and then looked where she was looking.

There was a huge African American in the doorway, dressed in blue jeans and a white Levi work-shirt. He stepped aside, and there was Walt Adams.

He looked beat and he looked drunk, but he was not yet so dirty as the rest of Skid Row. He slopped to an empty table and sat down, and a redheaded waitress toddled toward him on weak ankles.

There was no use going to all this trouble and then panicking him. I wanted to reason with Walt, not put the collar on him. I turned back and put another four bits out. 'Oil the lady, Mac.'

'Sure,' Olga said. 'I got dry bearings.'

The bartender laughed. At that, it was probably a funnier remark than he usually heard in a week; one of the sherry drinkers was telling the other how she had a rich uncle, if the old bastard would just take the rubber off his wallet; the

Green Death man was talking to himself, assuring himself he was the greatest pitcher in the big leagues.

We held our drinks in our hands, the thin smell of blended whiskey making me gag a little. Olga said: 'That fella there's a friend of mine. Okay if we talk to him a bitty minute?'

Playing it cool. I went along with her: 'Okay with me if it is with the man here. Can we take our glasses to the table?'

The bartender looked at me, and deadpan, said: 'You can take them if you're strong enough. You may take them for all of me. How the waitress feels about being beat from a tip, I dunno.'

So we joined Walt, and I signalled the redheaded waitress and ordered three. Olga said: 'It's good to see you, Walt.'

Walt Adams stared at her. 'It won't take hold,' he said. 'I've drunk and drunk, but it won't take hold.'

'Keep trying, boy.' This was me, with my two-and-a-half cents' worth.

Walt stared at me with the beginnings of hatred in his eyes. 'Andy the cop. St. Andrew the Upholder of the Righteous.

Come to arrest me, Andy?'

The girl brought our drinks. I paid her, tipped her the rest of a dollar, and she went away. All around us the sounds and the smells and the drab sights of Skid Row went on. At another table, a man was drinking a glass of tokay by bending over to it; his hands shook too hard to hold it.

Slowly, I said: 'It all depends, Walt. I couldn't do it without hearing your side first . . . After Ellie said you had a gun with you, I couldn't put out a bulletin and have some casual cop pick you up. He'd see the gun and shoot, and — ' I let him imagine the rest.

Some bravado came into his tired voice. 'Huh. Who'd shoot who? I've had that gun for a long time, sixteen years.'

Now it was my turn to be tired. 'You've been drinking. And how many times a year do you go out on a target range? You think a pistol aims itself?'

Olga drained her little jigger, set it down on the table with a thump. 'Stop it, Andy. Guns and violence, and who shoots who — that's no way to talk. You sound like a five-year-old boy playing television cowboy.'

Walt Adams said: 'Do you know, they operate on the actors before they make them cowboys? Remove all their brains but ten per cent.'

This was the Walt Adams who was our friend, my best friend in Naranjo Vista.

Olga saw it as quickly as I did. She said: 'Give Andy your gun, Walt.'

I said, fast: 'Pass it under the table. We don't want it seen in a place like this.'

'By God, no. A man's got the right to protect himself.'

Olga said: 'Andy threw away his protection for you. He's risked his job, our home, his career by not sending out word to pick you up.'

Walt said, suddenly: 'Could I have a cup of black coffee?'

I ordered it from the waitress. Olga switched her empty shot glass for mine. I wanted to tell her to knock off, to stop drinking, but I had better sense than to take a chance of losing her help.

The coffee came, a dime; I gave the girl a quarter. My eyes never left Walt's as I fumbled in my pocket for the coin and handed it out.

Walt Adams said: 'I could pull my gun on you and walk out. I could shoot you under the table, and in all this noise I could get away.'

'But you won't.'

'Why not? Andy, why not?'

Here we went. 'For the same reason that you didn't rape that Patterson girl.'

Olga gasped; Walt's breath went out in a sigh that carried waves of liquor to me, though I'd been drinking myself. He dumped his whiskey into his black coffee, and drank it in two gulps. His face seemed to pull together. 'I thought there was no such thing as a criminal type?'

'That's what every police officer says. And then, when a crime is committed, the first thing he does is run to the M.O. file, convinced that whoever did the crime is probably in the habit of committing that crime, and few others.'

The black coffee, lightly diluted with a half an ounce of light whiskey, had pulled him together; or maybe the steady talk was doing it. 'That's interesting. I guess it's interesting. So I'm not a rapist?'

'Olga thinks you're not, and she's a psychologist. Hal Levy thinks you're not, and he's your doctor. I'm just a dope, but I'm your friend. I'd rather think not.'

Anger flared in his tired face, and I shifted my weight, ready to hit him if I had to. But his anger was not for me; he said: 'Hal Levy has no right to give away his patient's secrets!'

Of course. Oh, of course. Dr. Levy hadn't meant that Walt Adams was too gentle a guy to commit rape; he had meant that Walt was impotent. I am always so damned slow that it irritates me; stupid is a better word. I have to make up for it with training and energy.

'Give me your gun, Walt.' Now I knew how to proceed. 'You'd rather be dead than have it come out in public, but it doesn't have to. I'm a good detective, Walt. Maybe the best you'll ever meet. Give me the gun, and then give me the facts, and I'll get this thing solved and broken without — without anything having to come out that isn't really involved.'

'You say.'

'I say.'

My eyes had never left his; now I saw him falter, waver, look hopeful. I was looking as self-confident as a girl who's just been crowned Miss America. But I didn't have a bathing suit on. I must remember to tell Olga my thoughts at that moment, the moment when something nudged my knee, and my hand closed around the butt of Walt Adam's pistol and snaked it into my belt, under my shabby coat.

My clever wife must have known what happened, because her voice was less tense, less professional as she said: 'What really happened, Walt?'

He shrugged a little. 'Do I have to go into it all? I mean about Ellie and me and then — '

'And then, Miss Crowthers and you,' I said, as he broke off. 'I knew about that. I took her home, she had a breakdown, and she was muttering your name. I found a picture of you in her drawer. But nobody knows about it except me and her headshrinker.'

'Professor Barnhart is a psychiatrist,' Olga said, automatically.

'That Patterson kid,' Walt said. 'My God, I've been a schoolteacher for years and years, and I never looked at a high school girl before as anything but a problem or a no-problem. But she was working in the office, and she kept brushing against me and — you know.

'She used to meet me out in the night. In my car, or out in the field, we had a blanket hidden out there. Twenty-five dollars a time, she did it for money. I felt like a pig, but a — an uncastrated pig.'

That wasn't bad, either. I said: 'Nineteen years old is not a kid, Walt.' I thought of some of the girls that age I'd known in occupied territory. I thought of myself, two years after I'd first enlisted. I'd put childish things far behind me by then.

'Then I couldn't do it with her any more, either,' Walt said. 'She laughed at me.'

There was a little island of silence in that raucous joint, a little island around our table. I'd stopped looking into Walt

257

Adams's eyes. I didn't know what to say. But Olga did. She put her hand on Walt's and said: 'We're not laughing, Walt.'

'She still wanted money,' Walt said. 'She'd kept little notes I'd passed her. What I am is humiliating enough for Ellie. To find out about the girl . . . I hit her,' he said, suddenly. 'She wanted more money than I could afford, and we met and I hit her, just a slap, and she scratched my face, and then I really socked her, and she went down. Down and out,' said Walt Adams.

'Did you choke her?' I asked.

'No. Why should I? She was knocked out, and Ellie was having this party, and I went back to the house. Hal Levy patched me up; I'd been socked by that gun-thug, Bailey Spratt, too.'

'If you hadn't you wouldn't have hit the girl,' my headshrinker wife said.

Walt Adams said: 'I suppose not.' Then he sank back into his apathy again. They always do that, after they confess; they sort of collapse, as though they'd reached the top of a steep hill.

I wanted to ask him if he'd told Hal

Levy about the girl. I started to, and then I realized that he hadn't; Levy was too much of a doctor not to have rushed right out and tended her.

'Simple assault,' I said. 'A punch in the jaw. Not much of a crime, Walt.'

He said suddenly: 'Olga, if you see Hal Levy, don't tell him I got mad at what he told Andy, here. He's been a damned good friend to me.'

'What did he do for you, Walt?'

Olga said, sharply: 'Andy, shut up!'

I shot my hand out and grabbed her thin wrist. 'You can be my girl, or you can be Hal Levy's girl, but you can't be both.'

She stared at me. This was not the way to talk to a wife you planned on keeping.

I doubt if Walt Adams had heard us. He said: 'When we got back from looking at — identifying — '

He was going to cry. I kept my voice as soft as possible, and said: 'I know where you were. What happened?'

Walt said, simply: 'I put myself in Hal Levy's hands. I told him I had hit Nora, but not raped her. He undressed me for bed and examined me and said he

259

wouldn't turn me in to the police. He was — I realize it — putting his whole professional career in my hands.'

'For which you've certainly repaid him,' Olga said.

I looked around the T-Star. This was the world, looked up at. From a doctor's office, it was the same world, but from the opposite point of view. I made my decision: 'Olga, you were a fool to marry a man as old as I am. Did you know I was beginning to get deaf?' I pushed back from the filthy table.

'Andy — ' My girl had tears in her fine eyes. But she was still my girl.

'Let's go,' I said. 'We're taking you home, Walt.'

Now I knew what I had to do. It would cost about forty-five cents and some gas. In Jack Davis's present mood, I'd be damned if I'd turn in a bill to the city; this would come out of my own pocket.

Slowly we walked back to our car. We passed bums and tramps, street walkers and dames that were just pub crawlers; uniformed cops and undercover men; hopheads and people who just smoked a little pot now and then. Humanity. A low stratum, but people; the ones I was sworn to protect.

As we passed the uniformed rookies, swinging their nightsticks, flaunting their guns, I wondered if any of them had yet realized the awful weight on a cop's shoulders, not at all offset by the weight of the gun on his hip.

From their unlined faces, I didn't think that the thought, or much of any thought, had bothered them. If it did, would they quit police work now, with their lives ahead of them?

Me, I couldn't quit. I was pushing forty, and I didn't know anything else. I could pump gas in a filling station, or pass out cigars in a drug store, but I couldn't make enough money to keep my house — and, I thought, my wife — any way but by wearing the old badge and gun.

We were almost at the parking lot. Where a liquor store window threw a bright patch of golden light on the sidewalk, I stopped. 'You two go ahead. I'll join you at the car.'

Walt Adams swung around and faced me. 'Go on, by myself?'

'You've run away once,' I said. 'You're too smart to repeat yourself.'

He stared at me, and a tiny, half-smile twisted his lips. Olga took his arm, and they walked on.

The liquor store had a phone on the wall, no booth. I bought a pint of the cheapest tokay before I used the phone to call the sheriff's office, back in our county seat. When I asked for the detectives, a Lieutenant Hansen answered. I told him who I was. 'I'm in Los Angeles. I'll be out there in an hour. Could you have a police stenographer and someone from the D.A.'s office meet me?'

Hansen said: 'Sure. What have you got, Bastian?'

'Crack in the Patterson case. Think we can wind it up tonight.'

My pockets bulky with the pint and with Walt Adams's gun, I went on to my car, paying the parking lot man as I went by. That was something I'd forgotten; I could park cars, too.

But this was a park-yourself lot. Olga

was behind the wheel, Walt Adams in the back seat. Olga asked me if I wanted to drive. I shook my head and got in beside her, and she started off smoothly, twisted in and out of traffic for a couple of blocks, and put us on the freeway, heading for the county seat and home.

I said: 'I owe your friend Levy an apology.'

'You apologize to Hal Levy and I'll — I'll put salt in your coffee.'

This brought me straight up in my seat. 'Hey, Olga, what are you mad about?'

'You put in seven hundred and twenty hours a week trying to keep our town running nicely, and then an educated floop like Hal Levy holds out on you — I suppose because good guys don't snitch — and almost ruins everything.'

I took this one thing at a time. 'An educated what?'

'A floop. Hal Levy is a floop.'

'Certainly wish I had your educated vocabulary . . . And there aren't seven hundred and twenty hours in a week.'

'Don't be any squarer than you have to.'

'Just a cube, that's me. Andy Bastian, square any way you look at me.'

She laughed a little. I looked in the back seat. Walt Adams was asleep. I put my chin down and rested, but I didn't shut my eyes. We left Los Angeles County, and, after a while, we crossed into our own. I was again on duty, as a sworn deputy. I told Olga to turn off for the County General Hospital.

She nodded, and made the switch. It was only about ten o'clock, though it felt like four in the morning; the big County General, looming beside the freeway, was still lit up.

'Back door,' I said, and showed her where to park, in the spaces reserved for police cars. Then I got out and walked away, and, after a second, walked back again and around to her side of the car.

The night was getting damp and chilly, but she had her window down; I had no trouble at all kissing her. In return, I got one of her grins; they had been a little rare, lately.

The police ward was familiar to me; we'd had a hit-and-run violator there for a few days. But the guard on the gate didn't know me. I had to show him my I.D. Then he stood aside, saluting, and I went through the barred gate and he locked me in.

A male nurse was on the desk. I asked him for Junior Wright. I had forgotten the first name again.

No one is more bored than a male nurse; I've never known one to show the slightest interest in anyone. This one went slowly through his whole list before he deigned to look at the Ws. Then he said: 'Sorry. Not here.'

'What do you mean, he's not here?'

'No Wright.' He picked up a temperature chart and examined it with intense, devoted interest, a scientist about to discover something to shake the medical world.

'He was here,' I said. 'Where did he go?'

He didn't look up. 'They come and they go. How should I know?'

'Who would?'

'Maybe Dr. Eastman. I'll turn his light on.' He pressed a button on his desk, and leaned back, exhausted.

Dr. Eastman was young, black-haired, thin-mustached, peppy. He was the man I'd talked to on the phone; his voice sounded older than he looked. When he heard my name, he said he was glad to see me.

'Where's my boy, doctor?'

'Flew away. A lawyer named Leonard came in with a habeas corpus, and I had to let him go.'

Of course. Junior had gotten over his aversion to his father and his father's lawyer. I said: 'Found out where they were taking him?'

Eastman grinned. 'There was a lot of talk about an ambulance plane to take him upstate. It occurred to me that you might not like that, so I waved my little learning around, and convinced them he'd be better off just riding one of our elevators to a private room.'

'Why, thanks. That's a high grade of cooperation.'

The grin twisted the hair-line mustache again. 'The police helped me through school,' he said. 'They gave me a job tending short-wave radios. I like cops. It may not be fashionable, but I am a copper-bug. Your little hunk of nothing is in Room 2332.'

'And thanks a lot.'

'Any time,' he said, and turned back toward the ward.

It was nice timing; the gate clanged just as his door closed, and my men were there. Lieutenant Hansen, big in plainclothes, and an assistant District Attorney he introduced as Mr. Norris.

When I told them our man had been moved to the twenty-third floor, we went out through the gate again. Hansen stopped to get his .38 back from the guard; it is improper and illegal to carry a firearm into a prison ward, just like a jail. I kept my mouth shut about my gun — and Walt Adams's — in my pocket. The guard had forgotten to ask me if I was armed.

The male nurse didn't look up to watch us go; we didn't exist for him. I wondered what possible good he did the county payroll sitting at that desk. It didn't seem to be any of my business.

An elevator took us down to the twenty-third, a walk took us to 2332. There was no Do Not Disturb or No Visitors sign on the door, for which I thanked my tiny luck.

There was no doctor or private nurse in attendance.

Junior Wright was there, all right, small in a big bed. The bandages around his ribs bulked up through the bedclothes; his eyes were bright with fever, and the stench of paraldehyde was strong in the room.

Hansen said: 'Let me know when to start writing,' and took a notebook out of his pocket.

I said: 'Hello, Junior.'

'Ya kin go t'hell,' he said. He was using his Skid Row accent.

'Now, Junior, I don't think we're going to do that.'

'Don't call me Junior.'

'Why not?' I asked. 'When you go into the gas chamber, don't you want everyone to read your real name in the papers? That'll really peeve your old man.'

'You can drop that hard-boiled cop talk,' he said. 'You don't have anything on me, or you wouldn't have let me out of that terrible prison ward.' He was being cultured for a while.

'With that crease on your ribs, you weren't going any place,' I said. 'I needed a little time to hang it on you, and here it comes. You raped that girl.'

'What you bin sniffin'?' Skid Row again.

'No sniff. Just a swallow.' I took the bottle of tokay out of my pocket, let its paper bag fall rustling to the floor.

The D.A., Mr. Norris, said: 'You can't give liquor to a prisoner.'

'If you want to get technical, he isn't a prisoner. After a while I'll book him, and then he won't get another drink for the rest of his life.'

Lieutenant Hansen said: 'Take it easy, Norrie, I think Bastian's onto something.' He still held his notebook and pencil, but he hadn't started writing again. It was obvious that this was no new scene to him. I wanted Junior to have time to think long, juicy thoughts, so I looked at

Lieutenant Hansen.

He had blue eyes, not surprising in a Hansen. But blue, gray, brown or black, all police eyes look the same, I thought. Hard and bright and not interested in anything at all.

I wondered if mine had that look. I hoped not.

And then I chuckled under my breath. Schizoid, in my wife's language. As two-way as little Junior, with his Skid Row-Ivy League personalities.

People who looked down on cops made me mad, and cops made me mad, and what did that make me? A poor, shorn lamb in a world of misunderstanding, a concept that hardly fitted my long, tough frame, the two guns in my pocket, or my background.

Junior Wright moved uncomfortably in the bed, and said: 'Whatta I got to do to get that vino? Like talk?'

'Like talk, Junior,' I said. 'About the girl. About everything that happened. What you were doing in Naranjo Vista, what you'd been doing, how you got there. And about the girl.'

'I never hit her,' Junior said. His tongue was thickening in his mouth. The sweat on his forehead was, I knew, cold; I didn't touch him to find out. Surely the nurses had bathed him, but I didn't want to touch him, anyway.

'No,' I said. 'You never hit her.' I put the bottle back in my pocket, and smiled at his horrible little face. 'You found her knocked out on the ground, before you ever got there.'

He blinked at me, running his tongue across his lips. Not being a drinking man, I had only a vague idea what he was going through. It looked horrible. 'You see,' I said, 'I know what happened. But you can save me a lot of trouble by admitting it.' I took the bottle out, and said: 'You may have one swallow.' I split the plastic seal with my thumbnail, took the screw cap off, let the sweet, heavy odor go up his nose. His Adam's apple was jerking like on a hooked trout, or a hanged man.

'She was on the ground,' he said. The lights in the pint bottle had him hypnotized. 'Her skirt was up.' He was using his Ivy League accent. Then he cracked. 'For God's sake, give me the drink, cap.'

Hansen was writing. I handed Junior the wine. He gulped, and would have gone on gulping, but I bent the bottle down, and took it away from him. Sticky wine ran down his chin, pursued by his too-short tongue. He brought a finger up, mopped the wine; licked the finger. The nurses had scrubbed his hands clean, but they hadn't been able to do much about his fingernails.

Taking my time, hamming it up, I screwed the cap back on the bottle. I started to slide it back into my pocket.

Junior's voice was almost a scream. 'Well, a guy sees a goody like that, you think he's gonna pass it up? Nice, clean girl, laying there, asking for it. I give it to her!' He grinned. 'She come to. She knew I was doing it, towards the end, and she liked it.' But his eyes were on my pocket. I gave him another snort.

Hansen looked up from his book and gave me a sour grin. We knew, we were cops, we'd been there before. They go all the way down below the gutter, but sexual pride goes with them; they have to pretend they can give a girl pleasure. The truth undoubtedly was that Junior Wright had never aroused a response in a woman in his life; and there was little doubt that Nora Patterson had been too far gone to respond to anything.

Back to dear Junior.

Business of drops down the chin, business of tongue and fingers all over again. I had had enough of this, but I was not being paid to quit when I had enough, but when the people did. The People, versus.

'What were you doing in Naranjo Vista?'

He shrugged, then winced; he'd hurt his ribs. 'Employment agency, state employment agency sent me out,' he said. 'I had the shorts, down to my last deemo.'

Hansen sighed and cut in. 'Deemo?'

'Dime,' Junior Wright said. 'A job washing cars. Supposed to be a buck an hour, but this guy wouldn't pay more'n fifty cents.'

'What was his name?'

'A big shot. They make it in wheelbarrow loads, but he wouldn't pay more'n fi'ty cents. I ain't no scab,' Junior Wright said, with dignity. 'I don't work for four bits the hour. He think I'm a bum?'

'His name?'

'Sprigg or Spratt or something.'

'Bailey Spratt?'

'I dunno. So I walked out on him. Now I'm in the boondocks, no money, can't even get to Skid Row, where maybe I can make a contact.'

They are generous on the Row, knowing each other's needs. They buy friendship on the Row, a pal for a swallow, a lifelong buddy for a pint. They mean it, at the time.

'I try the liquor store,' Junior Wright said. 'I'll wash his windows, scrub his floor, but it's no contact. I cannot make a buy,' Junior said, and his eyes were luminous with memory of his pain. 'There's nothing for it but the backyard route.' He shook his head. 'That's when I got the fright. You can't backyard it when you're in a town where everybody is in the right place.'

Norris was looking a question. I gave Junior Wright another swallow, and said: 'He means going along an alley, looking into kitchen windows till you see a bottle of cooking sherry.'

'Huh,' Junior said, licking his finger, 'beer in an ice-box, too. Who misses one?'

Hansen and I looked at each other. It was a thought. If a bum slipped into a kitchen, took a beer, and ran, who would ever know to report it? Each of us filed it away in our police minds. Sometime it would be valuable.

'Too much risk,' Junior Wright said. 'And then I see this Mr. Sprigg again. The one who wanted to pay me fifty cents an hour. I'm gonna pitch him the tale, tell him I've thought it over, anything to get a buck advance out of him. He's driving, but he is driving slow, like he's about to stop. And that he does, out by the golf course, like, and there's a girl, and she gets in with him, and they have a drink. I'm behind some trees. They drink out of a bottle, and he puts it in the glove compartment and they go into the trees and I come out, and get the bottle.'

275

His eyes were bright with the memory. Mine felt bright, too. From the dronings of Sunday-fools back in the Orphan Home, a phrase boiled up: 'Mine enemy is delivered into my hands.' I gave Junior Wright another snort.

'I'm awake when Mr. Spratt comes out of the woods and gets in his car,' Junior said, getting Bailey's name right for once. 'Then the girl is walking away, and I am taking a little nap. Then I wake up, and there's still two good snorts in the bottle. While I am repasting myself with those, the girl comes back.' He was lit, now; his language getting flossy and Skid Row elegant. 'She waits, smoking a cigarette. A guy comes along, walking. She throws her cigarette away. You should never throw a lighted butt away in the country,' Junior Wright said. 'It starts forest fires.'

The D.A., Norris, let out a snort, and concealed his face in the palm of his hand.

'Maybe they're gonna do it,' Junior Wright said, simply, 'and I like to watch. Anyway, Mr. Spigot's bottle is empty. I move over there, soft like a pussycat, just

276

as the guy socks her. She goes for his face, wow, wow, scratching away, and he socks her again, and she goes down, and he goes away, fast. I move in and look her over.'

A pretty picture was conjured up; Nora Patterson lying sprawled on her back, skirt up. And Junior Wright, filthy, reeking with stolen whiskey — he'd been lucky he could keep it down — looking her over, perhaps whinnying a little, certainly breathing hard.

'So I give it to her,' Junior Wright said. 'She'd maybe been asking this other guy, and he turns her down, but I'm right there. But I'm careful, I do it so she won't get a baby,' he said. 'This is a hell of a world to be a kid in,' said the man named Junior.

I gave him the bottle; this time I didn't pull it away. There was one more question, and the drunker he was, the better for my purposes.

Norris asked it: 'Could you identify the man who hit this girl?'

'Kinda fat,' Junior Wright said dreamily. He held a firm grip on the pint. It wasn't nearly enough for him, but he nursed the last inch in the bottom, sipping. Afterwards would come the paraldehyde again. 'About forty,' Junior Wright said. He liked being the center of all this attention now. The wine had drawn a blanket over his personal danger.

'Could it have been this Bailey Spratt?' I asked.

'Could be,' Junior Wright said. 'Could not be.' He drained the bottle, and I looked at Hansen and Norris.

'Enough,' Mr. Norris said.

But Junior had not had an audience like this in years.

'Whataya mean, Bailey Spratt?' Junior asked. 'I never heard of no Bailey Spratt. You're trying to put words into my mouth,' he wailed. 'It ain't fair.'

'The man who wanted you to wash cars.' My voice was its most patient. I didn't feel that way myself.

'His name was Luther Schmidt,' Junior Wright said, with great clarity.

'And he was a new car dealer in Naranjo Vista?' Junior crouched under the whip of my voice; Norris and Hansen were looking at me curiously.

'I never said that,' Junior cried. Tears were running down his scrubbed — by the nurses — face. 'He's like a used-car dealer an' bus operator over in Citrus Grove. I was walkin' back through Naranjo Whatsit, tryin' for a back door.'

My breath came ripping out so hard that I choked and coughed. Mine enemy was no longer in my hands. I had seen Luther Schmidt's sign driving by Citrus Grove, which was the next subdivision over.

Norris and Hansen were still looking at me. If they had been my men, would I have tried to bully Junior into changing his story a little bit, and naming Bailey Spratt? I don't know.

'We've got enough,' Mr. Norris said again.

I nodded slowly.

'I'll type it up fast in the nurse's office, and get him to sign it,' Hansen said. 'Even with three witnesses, it's better to get them to sign it.'

I said that it certainly was always better to get them to sign it, and shook hands all around, and we walked down the hall.

Hansen asked the floor nurse if he could use her typewriter. Before sitting down to it, he hitched his gun out of the way so it wouldn't stick into his prosperous belly. He carried an awful lot of gun barrel for a plainclothes man.

Riding down in the elevator, Norris asked me what I thought.

'What do you lawyers say? *Nolle prosequi*?'

'That's the noun,' Norris said, sourly. 'The verb is '*nol pros.*' You think we have no case?'

'Depends,' I said. 'I've got an awful lot of stuff, too. This Patterson girl was running it hot and heavy, for money. Middle-aged men are fools for the teen-age stuff.'

'Nineteen,' Mr. Norris said. 'Well above the age of consent.'

'There's still contributing to the delinquency of a minor,' I said. 'A high misdemeanor, if not a felony. There's still the simple old fact that a guy who has been laying a high school girl wouldn't want his wife to know about it. Taxpayers, friends. I've uncovered two guys she was selling it to, but I'll bet there were five or six.'

We were at the bottom. We walked out to the parking lot. I could make out the dim figures of Olga and Walt in my car. I did not want Mr. Norris to meet Walt.

He said: 'One thing certain. We would never get to prosecute the girl for blackmail. Don't know that I'd want to. She's had enough. Imagine her family'll move away and leave this county in peace and quiet. Wright, upstairs? I understand his old man's rich.'

'Yes. He brought a lawyer down from Stockton. Shyster named Leonard.'

Mr. Norris let out a big sigh, aimed at the stars, which were invisible in the smog that had started to bless us again. 'Leonard's no shyster. A very successful banker-and-broker attorney. Surprised he'd step into a criminal affair; means Wright Senior is really loaded. Well, that does it. The girl was unconscious but how do we prove a thing like that? Junior says she opened one eye and winked at him, and who's to prove she didn't?'

'He said she wasn't conscious till towards the end.'

'He'll lie better,' Mr. Norris said. 'Have a cigarette? Yes, he'll lie better when his lawyer tells him we have to prove she was unconscious. Which we can't.'

We lit up. In the glow, his face was strained and serious. 'You're lucky, being a cop,' he said. 'All you have to do is arrest the right man. Me, us, the prosecutors, we have to block all the loopholes, and if we don't, we have to figure we're turning all kinds of criminals loose, letting them laugh at the law.'

My smoke curled up in front of me. It was a very still night, down where we were, but there must have been air currents up above; the smog smelled of Fontana, twenty miles away. 'Considering the sort of girl Nora Patterson is, it would be a shame to sock Junior Wright with a rape charge.'

'How about the next girl he finds — No, that's silly. A man doesn't stumble on two girls like that in a lifetime.'

'No,' I said. 'A man doesn't find two girls like that in a lifetime. But it seems a lousy shame that Junior goes free as an eagle in a windstorm. It is sort of an insult to your profession, and mine, and to every decent citizen in the whole damned United States.'

'Any suggestions, lieutenant?'

We were two sworn officers of the law, but we were alone in a dark parking lot. We couldn't see each others' eyes, at least I couldn't see his. I said: 'Mr. Leonard is a civil lawyer, he wouldn't know much about criminal courts and criminal charges. Think he'd fall for a bluff?'

Mr. Norris said: 'Till I hear what the bluff is, I couldn't say.'

The next step up for him was as an elective officer, not appointed as cops are. Junior's father had money. Money comes in handy when you're running for office. I said: 'Offer to let Junior go if he will sign a voluntary commitment to a state mental institution. For drying out, for mental therapy.'

Mr. Norris teetered on his heels. He locked his hands behind his back, and looked up, consulting the smog-hidden stars. 'It would sound very, very good,' he said. 'Yes. I do the Wrights a favor. And I do the community one, too.' He chuckled. 'And poor Junior. There's one hospital, I have to look up to see which one, where the doctors believe in a wino quitting cold turkey, no tapering off at all. I'll make it that one.'

'He'll at least not be any trouble to any cops for a while. What's left of the case, Mr. Norris?'

'How about the man who knocked Norma Patterson out? A thousand dollars, six months in county jail, there.'

'For socking a blackmailer, male or female?'

Mr. Norris waved smoke away from in front of him. 'If we're so damned prosperous,' he asked, 'why can't we get air to breathe? No fun smoking in this stuff.' He ground his cigarette out, viciously. 'Yeah, I guess I sympathize with the guy, even though I was brought up never to sock a lady . . . I'm past forty myself. It could be an awful temptation.'

'I'm in my late thirties,' I said.

'Watch it, in a couple of years,' Mr. Norris said. He put out his hand again, and we separated.

16

We didn't talk on the way home. But when I stopped in front of Walt Adams's house, he didn't get out. I reached across Olga and gave him a shove. 'Go to bed. You need your rest.'

'Did you put up bail for me?'

'The trouble with this country is, everybody reads detective stories. You can't have bail unless you've been arraigned; you can't be arraigned till you've been arrested; you shouldn't be — this isn't always true — arrested till you've committed a crime. And you have, Walt, you have. You socked a student, and that is something teachers shouldn't do, but since you did it on your own time, the D.A. is going to forget it. Good night.'

He stumbled out of the car, and stood there in the glow of a street lamp. 'What'll I tell Ellie?'

'Good God, Walt, I haven't been married long enough to learn to lie to

Olga yet. She always catches me.'

Olga chuckled, and then Walt turned and started walking toward his house. I'd almost forgotten something. I called him back. 'You have to get rid of Miss Crowther.' He nodded. 'A classmate of mine has been looking for an assistant principal. In Montana . . . '

I drove to our house.

I was getting into my best uniform when Olga came into the bedroom with our largest cup, full of coffee. 'What happened?' she asked.

So I told her. 'At least two felonies, and a flock of misdemeanors,' I said. 'Rape by Junior Wright, blackmail by Norma Patterson, two adulteries, an assault and battery. Not a prosecution in the lot.'

She said: 'And Naranjo Vista remains un-smirched.'

'No. The Patterson case got in the papers. It'll be dropped, now, and people will forget, but if you think I did all this to keep Mr. Bartlett's investment safe, you — '

'I think you've committed a little adultery, too. What you've done to law and order verges on the sexual.'

'Huh?' Then I got it. All I had to do was translate it into four letter words. They come easier to me, anyway. 'I'll go along with the gag, Olga. Maybe I screwed law and order, but I ended up making love to justice. I've always had a yen for the old lady, anyway.'

She sat down at the foot of the bed, and watched me tie my black silk tie. In the mirror I could see her nodding. 'But when Hal Levy did the same thing, you were sore as hell.'

'Hal Levy is too damned good looking to be my wife's partner. I was looking for an excuse to slough him.'

Now she was grinning, the good old Olga grin. 'Okay, loot. You win. I'm going to medical school. Four years from now, I'll start looking for a good-looking partner.'

'Pick a lady osteopath. Four years from now I'll be ready for a little gentle massage.'

She got up, took my uniform coat off the chair where I'd hung it, brushed some dust off one elbow. 'You going to tell me why the Class A garb at midnight?'

'Bailey Spratt,' I said.

I left her laughing.

Dressed in my best uniform, I walked into what I persisted in thinking of as a police station, instead of a Civic Security Center. Not at all to my surprise, I found Captain Jack Davis there, chatting with the desk sergeant.

We walked to his office. He said: 'Hansen called me from up at the sheriff's office. You've done a nice piece of work, Andy.'

'By bluff and gall. How's our vigilante situation?'

Jack Davis clucked. 'We now got two police headquarters. This one, and one at Bailey Spratt's house. So, all right, say I told you so. You wanted to sock those amateurs hard, and all I could remember was that they were among the most important guys in our town. What now?'

'Check it to me, Jack?'

'Hell, yes, Andy.'

'I'm bluffing good tonight. I got two things on Bailey Spratt. I think I can bluff him quiet. With a pair of treys. Trey one

— you use that confession I got out of his kid?'

'Certainly not,' Jack Davis said. His big red hands jerked at his desk drawer, drew out the three papers I'd had the high school boys sign. 'They're not worth a thing,' Jack said. 'The kids were scared of the big policeman. You threatened to beat them. Yeah, yeah, I know you didn't, but just your size and your position has been ruled as being terrifying. If you'd had a juvenile officer from the court present, they might — repeat, might — stand up.'

'I've been threatening winos and consorting with fugitives,' I said. 'And buying drinks while wearing a gun, in violation of the penal code. I'm an outlaw, daddy-o, as no doubt no kid ever said. Gimme that paper, and I'll try one last bluff. After all, you have a pre-dated resignation from me.'

'Don't talk like a cheesewit. I need you around here. You said you had a pair of threes. What's the other one?'

'It's a pretty limp card,' I admitted. 'But my luck's in. Maybe. Did Hansen tell you that Junior saw this Luther

Schmidt lay the Patterson girl . . . ? Schmidt's in the car business, so is Bailey Spratt. Those guys all know each other. As you've found out if you tried to turn a car in. Think a big salesman type like Schmidt could keep from telling another big salesman type like Spratt that there was a twenty-five buck, nineteen-year-old piece in Spratt's town?'

Jack Davis stared at me. Finally he said: 'There's something to be said for living with a psychologist, after all.'

'Don't bandy my wife's name around your filthy police station.'

We stared at each other. I don't remember who started laughing first. When we stopped, Jack Davis said: 'I thought it was damned funny Walt Adams and Bailey Spratt would slug each other over the high school gun team. The girl had told Walt she'd gotten a proposition from Spratt.'

'You know, I never thought of that,' I said. 'Sure. If Walt didn't come up with some money, she was going to give her darling self to Bailey. Spratt's the kind of guy Walt would really hate.'

Jack Davis said: 'I ain't about to offer to adopt him, my own self. You got a white thread on your sleeve, Andy. I want you should look real good over at Mr. Spratt's house.'

So I left him the thread for a souvenir.

Driving to Bailey Spratt's I passed several cars on slow patrol. Amateurs.

The guy who answered my ring was just a kid. He was, for heaven's sake, in the uniform of corporal of the Civil Air Patrol, the semi-military outfit that teaches kids ground control and aircraft maintenance and radio and so on. He had a .38 revolver strapped around his waist, in a highly-tailored holster and belt. He wore it quick draw fashion, on the left side, butt forward.

I snapped: 'Corporal, that is a military uniform you have on. That gun is not G.I. It should be a .45 automatic, and it should be worn in a neat and military position. Take it off!'

He said: 'Yes, sir,' because I had spoken that way. Of course, I had no authority in Bailey Spratt's house to tell anyone to take off an unconcealed weapon. I said:

'Take me to Mr. Spratt.' Your leader.

'This way, sir.' His ears were a pair of Harvard beets going ahead of me.

Old Bailey really had himself a setup. He had two more CAP kids working a short-wave radio; he himself was behind an ornately-carved Spanish desk, dressed in his sheriff's posse uniform. The belt alone would have cost me a week's salary.

I said: 'Why the Air Force, Spratt? You going to bomb Los Angeles?'

He had the sense to blush a little. 'These boys are radiomen,' he said. 'One of them repairs car radios for me. It was their own idea to wear their uniforms.'

'No matter,' I said. 'Go on home, kids. I hope that's your own transceiver you are using. I'm Military Intelligence, and I'd hate to have to tell the Air Force their equipment was being misappropriated.'

'It's my set, sir,' the kid at the controls said.

'Okay, then. Just issue an over-and-out: all posse patrol cars will be off the streets in five minutes. Thereafter, they'll be held for inciting to riot. I mean, their drivers will.'

Bailey Spratt grinned at my slip. He said: 'I'm giving the orders here,' in a non-grinning voice.

The radio kid looked from one to the other of us, uncertainly. He must have been the one who worked for Bailey.

It was all very military; there was even a daybook lying on the desk in front of Gruppenfuehrer Spratt. I turned it around, picked up a ballpoint and wrote across it: 'I've been reading Nora Patterson's diary. A high misdemeanor, contributing to the delinquency of a minor.'

Bailey Spratt looked down at what I'd written. Then he slapped the book shut with two sweeps of his big hands, and said: 'Kids, go on home, and thank you. The lieutenant here has cleaned up the case. Everything is okay.'

He could think fast enough when he had to.

The boy at the controls plugged in, and said: 'Headquarters to all cars. Cease patrol, return to your homes. Over and — '

'Add: By order of the police to that.'

He did, and this time got over and out and started to take his set down. Bailey Spratt said: 'Let that go, Pete. Come over tomorrow and get it. Doesn't matter if you don't get to the shop till noon.'

The boy muttered something about being up to his neck in repairs, but there was something in Bailey Spratt's face that stopped him. He and his two friends left. When their car started, I could hear the voom of twin pipes, which are illegal in our town. I didn't chase after them to give them a ticket.

Then we were alone. Bailey Spratt stared at me across his desk. He had gotten his composure back. He said: 'Boys like that ought to have respect for authority. No use letting them hear two leaders fighting each other. Now, what you got to say?'

He hadn't asked me to sit down. But I went and got a chair and brought it over and put it opposite his desk, and sat down, and crossed my knees. I took plenty of time to do it, too.

Bailey Spratt said: 'You trying to

blackmail me, lieutenant? My friend the sheriff — '

'Your friend isn't coming out in favor of adultery, with an election in the future.'

Neither of us smiled.

I took it on. 'The Patterson girl will talk. We're not going to push charges. You weren't the only one. She was rolling over for anybody who had the money.'

His face was red, again.

While I had him off-balance, before he could raise enough anger to overcome his common sense, I played my second card. I slapped his son's confession down on the closed daybook. He looked at its few words.

'You'll look hot,' I said. 'A great big civic leader who can't control his own son. Who doesn't know what's going on in his own house. Who chases high school girls.'

I had to put it that way; I wasn't sure whether he'd connected with Nora or only gotten to the negotiating stage.

Bailey Spratt said: 'Does this have to get in the papers?' He pushed at the kid's confession with a fingertip. I remembered all he'd said about law and order and running the break-and-entry criminals out of town and away for life. He'd been talking about his own son, and hadn't known it.

'Everything's going to be all right,' I said. 'That is, if you listen to me.' Didn't he know juvenile crime was privileged, that no paper could print a j.d.'s name? Apparently not. Well, I didn't know the turn-in value of a 1949 Ford.

'Go ahead, lieutenant,' he said. Then he perked up, but just a little. My treys were standing up like aces.

'Not that I'm scared,' he said. 'But my son's future is at stake.'

'You're resigning from the sheriff's posse,' I said. 'Let someone else be the president of the gun club. Run your automobile business, and leave the guns to people who can carry them without losing their brains.'

The big man was quiet. 'And if I don't?'

'We're not pressing charges against you,' I said again. 'But we need to know the facts. A starchamber inquiry at the police station. No reporters present, just the principals. Norma Patterson and her parents. The other men involved with her. Their wives. You. Your wife.'

He flinched. I don't think it was love; he didn't love anything but the image of himself with a big gun on his hip. But alimony, now ——

'Then, a transcript would go to juvenile court. If the judge thinks an offender comes from an improper or immoral home, he could hold your boy till he was twenty-one.'

'I don't see —— '

'Just call it personal pique,' I said, and I started to get up. 'You tried to take this city away from the police, with your vigilantes. We resent that.' There was no use telling him he didn't have stability enough to carry a gun; we were removing his badge and his uniform, and that would have to do, the law being what it was.

'I said: 'If you want, we can take this up with the sheriff tomorrow, you and I.'

'I've only met the sheriff a couple of times, at barbecues and dinners,' Bailey

Spratt said. His son had looked better, in the high school office.

I was on my feet. Time to go. If I stayed and watched him as he now was, humiliated and crushed, I'd make a real enemy. I couldn't afford to.

The wind had come down to ground level at last, it was cool and fresh in the streets. I could almost smell salt air, but the ocean was a long ways away, I looked at my watch. One-thirty.

Tomorrow I had the duty at eight o'clock, and I would have to take time to see Nora Patterson and put the fear of God into her. Maybe I wouldn't have to tell her parents.

But I would, or they'd be spending money looking for the fiend who raped their stainless daughter. Their stainless-steel daughter.

That got a self-appreciatory grin out of me. But it would be a lousy interview. Also, I'd have to get some sort of release from Junior Wright and his lawyer, so they wouldn't sue Norman Patterson for shooting Junior. That would be easy, a swap for not prosecuting Junior, but it would take time.

A heavy day tomorrow. Time to go home to my medical student wife.

We do hope that you have enjoyed reading this large print book.

Did you know that all of our titles are available for purchase?

We publish a wide range of high quality large print books including:
Romances, Mysteries, Classics
General Fiction
Non Fiction and Westerns

Special interest titles available in large print are:
The Little Oxford Dictionary
Music Book, Song Book
Hymn Book, Service Book

Also available from us courtesy of Oxford University Press:
Young Readers' Dictionary
(large print edition)
Young Readers' Thesaurus
(large print edition)

For further information or a free brochure, please contact us at:
Ulverscroft Large Print Books Ltd.,
The Green, Bradgate Road, Anstey,
Leicester, LE7 7FU, England.
Tel: (00 44) **0116 236 4325**
Fax: (00 44) **0116 234 0205**

MYSTERY OF THE RUBY

V. J. Banis

According to legend, the Baghdad ruby has the power to grant anything the heart desires. But a curse lies upon it, and all who own the stone are destined to die tragically, damned for eternity. When Joseph Hanson inherits the gem after his uncle's bizarre murder, his wife Liza is afraid. Though his fortune grows, he becomes surly and brutal. And suddenly Liza knows there's only one way to stave off the curse of centuries — she must sacrifice her own soul to save the man she loves.

LONELY BUSINESS

Steven Fox

Herbie Vore, mystery writer and recent widower, leads a lonely, uneventful existence — until he begins to receive threatening postcards and packages referring to Cindy, his crush from long ago. When a teenager arrives at his door claiming to be the son of his old flame, Herbie learns that Cindy has also been receiving mysterious notes and phone calls. Who could want to harm them after all these years — and why? The investigation will uncover more than Herbie ever imagined — and possibly cost him his life . . .

TREACHERY IN THE WILDERNESS

Victor Rousseau

Joe Bostock and his chief engineer Will Carruthers are engaged on building a railway line in the wilds of Manitoba that will open up rich wheat lands for settlers — but the Big Muskeg swamp seems likely to ruin the construction scheme. When an unseen assailant treacherously picks Joe off with a rifle, Will, although wounded himself, vows to complete the railroad and bring his friend's murderer to justice. But he is hampered and his life threatened at every turn by a crooked syndicate led by a rival contractor . . .

MR. MIDNIGHT

Gerald Verner

Gordan Cross, crime reporter for the *Daily Clarion*, is detailed to discover the identity of a man known as Mr. Midnight, the mastermind behind a series of robberies and murders. Acting on a tip, he investigates The Yellow Orchid nightclub — and meets a variety of odd and suspicious people, including two who quickly turn up dead. How is the classy club implicated in the Midnight business — and who is the mysterious informant, 'A. Smith'? Teamed with Superintendent Budd of Scotland Yard, Gordan is determined to uncover the truth.

HAUNTED HELEN

V. J. Banis

Mentally scarred by her parents' violent deaths, Helen Sparrow was sent for treatment at a residential psychiatric clinic. Now discharged, she returns to a shadowy old mansion, the scene of both the murders and her repressed, unhappy childhood. But she senses an evil presence in the house: something that follows her along the gloomy halls and whispers just on the edge of her consciousness. Is she insane? Or does some supernatural echo of that terrible night lurk within those walls?